MY D

"Kate, can you
with me for a mi
approached my c
"Sure," I answe
we sat down side on the second step.

"It sure is a pretty night," I said as we watched the moon's silver reflection on the lake.

"I've never known a night that isn't beautiful out here on Lake Vallecito," Stony replied.

"You love it here, don't you?" I said softly.

Stony nodded. "I think this place has got to be as close to heaven as you can get." He laughed self-consciously. "I guess that sounds sort of stupid."

"No, it doesn't," I protested. "When Mom and Dad first told me we were coming here, I was really disappointed. I'd wanted to go to the beach in California. I had no idea it would be so beautiful here." *And I had no idea I'd meet somebody like you,* I added silently.

"Lake Vallecito has always been my favorite place," Stony finally replied. "But I especially like it right now." He laughed softly, and pulled me close to him. His lips slowly met mine in a kiss so warm and sweet that it left me breathless. . . .

BANTAM SWEET DREAMS ROMANCES

1 P.S. I LOVE YOU
3 LAURIE'S SONG
4 PRINCESS AMY
6 CALIFORNIA GIRL
7 GREEN EYES
8 THE THOROUGHBRED
9 COVER GIRL
10 LOVE MATCH
121 ONLY MAKE BELIEVE
140 LOVE DETOUR
143 CRAZY FOR YOU
145 THIS TIME FOR REAL
148 RIDDLES OF LOVE
149 PRACTICE MAKES PERFECT
150 SUMMER SECRETS
151 FORTUNES OF LOVE
152 CROSS COUNTRY MATCH
153 THE PERFECT CATCH
154 LOVE LINES
155 THE GAME OF LOVE
156 TWO BOYS TOO MANY
157 MR PERFECT
158 CROSSED SIGNALS
159 LONG SHOT
160 BLUE RIBBON ROMANCE
161 MY PERFECT VALENTINE
162 TRADING HEARTS
163 MY DREAM GUY

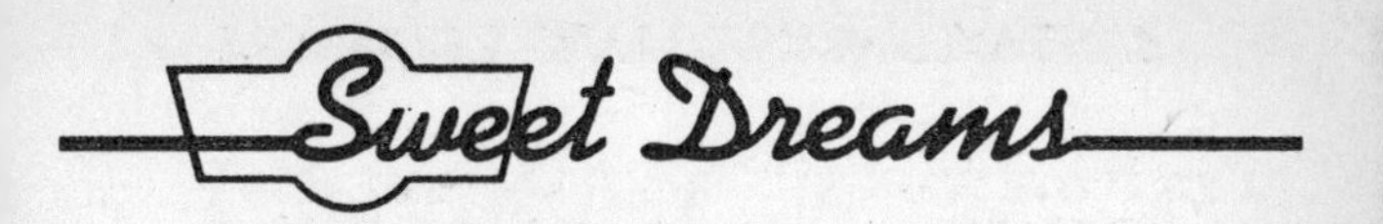

MY DREAM GUY

Carla Bracale

BANTAM BOOKS

NEW YORK • TORONTO • LONDON • SYDNEY • AUCKLAND

RL 6, IL age 11 and up

MY DREAM GUY
A Bantam Book / December 1990

Sweet Dreams and its associated logo are registered trademarks of Bantam Books, a division of Bantam Doubleday Dell Publishing Group. Inc. Registered in U.S. Patent Office and elsewhere.

Cover photo by Pat Hill.

ISBN 0-553-28173-9

Published simultaneously in the United States and Canada

Bantam Books are published by Bantam Books, a division of Bantam Doubleday Dell Publishing Group, inc. Its trademark, consisting of the words "Bantam Books" and the portrayal of a rooster, is Registered in U.S. Patent and Trademark Office and in other countries. Marea Registrada, Bantam Books, Inc., 666 Fifth Avenue, New York, New York 10103.

Printed and bound in Great Britain by
BPCC Hazell Books
Aylesbury, Bucks, England
Member of BPCC Ltd.

To Mom and Dad B.
&
Mom and Dad C.

Chapter One

"Lake Vallecito!" I stared at my parents in horror. "Why are we going *there* for vacation?"

My parents, my brother and I were sitting at the dinner table when my father dropped the bombshell. I put down my fork, my appetite totally destroyed.

"We've rented a beautiful cabin at Lake Vallecito. We'll be right on the shore of the lake for ten whole days," Dad explained, looking extremely pleased about the idea. "If we're lucky, we'll have fresh trout every night for supper!"

"But—I thought it was all planned. I thought we were going to California!" I knew my voice had a slightly hysterical edge to it, but I couldn't help it. I'd really been looking forward to spending my vacation at the Pacific Ocean. I'd bought a dynamite new bathing suit and had fantasized about some handsome blond lifeguard type falling madly in love with me. Desperately, I turned to my seventeen-year-old brother Jeff for support. "Jeff, tell the truth, wouldn't you rather go to the beach?"

Jeff shrugged his broad shoulders. "It doesn't matter to me. Lake Vallecito sounds okay. I guess I could learn to surf another time." He shoveled another forkful of mashed potatoes into his mouth.

I shot him my best "you traitor" look. Most of the time I think Jeff is pretty cool for a brother, especially considering he's almost two years older than me. Oh, he can be a real pain in the neck, always teasing me and driving me crazy, but most of the time I like him. At the moment, however, I could have cheerfully strangled him. He knew how important a vacation at the beach was to me!

"But I thought our plan to spend a week on the beach in California was definite," I persisted, unable to believe that my parents were changing our vacation plans two days before it was time to leave. "It's so unfair!"

My mother looked at me patiently. "Kate, I would like to spend some time in the Bahamas, but we don't always get what we want out of life. We were hoping we'd have the money for the trip to California, but things just didn't work out. Instead, we'll be going to Lake Vallecito, and I'm sure we'll all have a wonderful time." My mother's words were pleasant, but her tone of voice was one I recognized—the subject was closed.

"Well, I'm going to take the car down to the garage and see about getting an oil change and a tune-up. None of us will have any fun if the car breaks down." Dad stood up from the table and grabbed the car keys that hung on the kitchen wall. "I'll be back soon." He kissed my mom goodbye, then went out to the garage.

"And I've got to go change my clothes. I'm supposed to pick up Ralph in fifteen minutes. We're going to go see the Eddie Murphy movie playing down at the Bijou." Jeff also stood up and disappeared into his room.

I looked down at the piece of meat loaf left on my plate, depressed over my dream vacation that had turned to dust. Lake Vallecito was only about a five-hour drive from where we lived in Denver, and even though I'd never been there before, I had no desire to go now. I felt like my folks had offered me a whole cake, then given me just a crumb! I had spent more time than I cared to admit fantasizing about all the surfers I would meet in sunny California. I'd imagined the perfect scenario—white, sandy beaches, the bright blue ocean, beautiful sunsets, and one special guy at my side.

My mother's voice broke into my daydream. "Honey, I know you're disappointed about our vacation. It would have been fabulous to visit California, but it just isn't realistic this year."

Mom smiled at me understandingly. "You'll have a good time at Lake Vallecito. Your father and I went there on a vacation about twelve years ago. The cabins are really quaint and the scenery is breathtaking. There are gorgeous pine trees and huge, awesome mountains."

I looked at my mom in disbelief. How could she even begin to compare the scenery of Lake Vallecito to that of a California beach? How could she compare stupid pine trees to gorgeous, tanned hunks in swim trunks. Besides, what was so great about the mountains? I could see the mountains every day just by walking out in my front yard! And did she really think we communicated better when she used the word "awesome"?

"Besides, I want to stop at some of the antique stores on the way to the lake," Mom continued, "and see if I can pick up some things for the store."

"Oh, Mom, that's so boring!" I groaned. "I thought this was supposed to be a vacation, not a business trip!" There is nothing my mom loves more than puttering around cracked old dishes, musty-smelling furniture, and other stuff that she considers to be antiques. I, personally, would describe it as junk—ancient stuff that people paid a fortune to own!

"Kate, you know I'm so busy running my own antique store every day, I never get the opportunity to browse at other shops. Not only do I need to keep an eye out for interesting items, but I genuinely enjoy antiquing—for me that's going to be the best part of the vacation." She patted my hand briskly. "I promise I won't take up too much of your vacation time with my antique shopping. And I'm sure we're all going to have a wonderful vacation." She smiled at me and stood up. "Now, come on and help me clean up the kitchen."

"Uh, Mom, I promised Marcia I'd help her clean out her room," I protested. "Marcia's mom said that if Marcia doesn't clean out her closet by tomorrow morning, she's going to call the Salvation Army and have them take everything away!" This was really only half true. Marcia's mom had been saying the same thing for the last two months, so Marcia didn't take the threat too seriously. I hadn't promised Marcia that I'd help her, either, but I needed to get out of the house before anybody said one more word about my ruined vacation! Even though I knew deep down I was being obnoxious, I felt much too resentful to do the dishes!

"Well, all right, run along," Mom said, gathering up dishes from the table. "Just be home before dark."

I nodded and ran to my room to call Marcia before Mom had a chance to change her mind. Quickly, I grabbed the phone and punched in

Marcia's number. "Meet me at the usual place," I said when Marcia answered.

"Gotcha," said Marcia, and we hung up.

The usual place is a tree house at the back of Marcia's yard. Marcia's dad built it years ago and Marcia and I had spent lots of time up there playing house. We outgrew the dolls and tea parties long ago, but the tree house is still our favorite place for private discussions on the injustices of being a teenager.

I ran down the block, past the four houses that separate our two homes. When I reached Marcia's house, I went directly to the backyard and climbed up the five rungs that led to the tree house.

"So, what's so important that you drag me away from *Wheel of Fortune*?" Marcia was sitting in her usual spot on an old beanbag chair that was missing half its beans. Before I answered, I took my usual place, sitting cross-legged in the wicker chair that had no legs.

"What's going on is that my summer is ruined!" I exploded. "The trip to California is off."

"Off? Oh, wow, what a bummer," Marcia said sympathetically.

I nodded. "We're going to Lake Vallecito instead. I guess I'll be fishing instead of surfing," I said, trying to sound funny instead of glum.

For a moment neither one of us said anything. I didn't have to tell Marcia how disappointed I was about the change in our vacation plans. My best friend ever since second grade, Marcia Daniels knows everything about me.

"I can't believe it," I exclaimed. "I've been looking forward to seeing California for at least a month now—ever since school let out. We were going to fly there and everything!" I grabbed a leaf off the floor of the tree house and began to shred it. "Now all I have to look forward to is a five-hour car ride and ten days at a stupid lake!"

"Don't feel too bad. We're going to spend a week at my grandpa's place in the mountains for our vacation this year!" Marcia complained. "I guess that's part of the problem of living in Denver. With the mountains right here, it's easy for our parents to plan a scenic vacation without leaving the state."

"Yeah, I see what you're saying," I replied glumly. "But the scenery I'm interested in has nothing to do with mountains."

Marcia nodded in silent agreement. "You know," she said thoughtfully, "in some ways I hate summers. We don't see our friends every day like we do during the school year."

I sighed again, thinking about what she had said, "There is no way we're going to get any dates if this keeps up. This summer is by far the worst of our lives."

"We're too young to drive to places where the action is . . ." Marcia said.

"And too old to have tea parties and play with dolls to pass the time," I added, and Marcia and I looked at each other in perfect understanding. "I was really hoping I'd meet someone during my vacation." I leaned my chin in my hand. "Here I am, just turned sixteen years old, and I've never really been in love. Mom keeps telling me that love will eventually find me, but I'm beginning to think that love has lost my address!" I shredded the last of the leaf in my hand and looked back at Marcia. "And now it looks like all I'm going to meet is a bunch of fish!"

Marcia giggled, and shoved a strand of her long brown hair behind her ear. "At least the fish would kiss better than Jason Wallace."

I grinned at her at the mention of Jason. "You have to admit, Jason is really a hunk to look at. How was I supposed to know he's the grossest kisser in the world!" I giggled at the memory. "You know, it's a shame, too. I was really getting to like him before he kissed me. But I just don't see a future in that relationship." My grin widened as I looked at Marcia. "I tried to warn you about him, but you wouldn't believe me. You had to go out with him too and find out for yourself!"

"How was I supposed to know that was the one time in your life you weren't exaggerating," Marcia teased.

"I don't exaggerate a lot!" I protested.

Marcia looked at me sarcastically. "What

about that time last year when you were making dinner for your family and you called me and told me you thought you'd cut off your thumb while chopping vegetables?"

I flushed and grinned at her guiltily. "Okay, so that was a bit of an exaggeration," I admitted.

"Or last year when you told me you were sure that your brother was a spy because—"

"Okay, okay," I interrupted her before she could say anything more. "I admit it—sometimes I have an overactive imagination!"

"Sometimes?" Marcia snorted in disbelief.

"Yeah, but have you ever thought that maybe we're such good friends because I have so much imagination and you have none?" I grinned at Marcia.

"No, that's not why we're best friends," Marcia countered. "We're best friends because we're the exact same size and coloring and can borrow each other's clothes." Marcia laughed, her hazel eyes sparkling brightly. "And we became best friends in second grade because we thought we were long-lost sisters!"

I laughed, as always feeling better after talking to Marcia. "That's because we looked so much alike; we both had long brown hair and we always dressed the same."

"We looked alike *before* you cut your hair and developed such weird taste in clothes," Marcia teased. "Oh, that reminds me, do you still want to borrow my blue sundress for your vacation?"

I thought of the really cute blue sundress Marcia had said I could borrow for my fun-filled California trip. It really looked good on me and I'd thought it would be perfect for long, romantic walks on the beach.

"No, there's no point in wasting a perfect dress on a bunch of fish and wildlife." Once again I felt myself sliding into a depression.

"Kate, it might not be so bad. Maybe you'll meet a really gorgeous hunk," Marcia offered. "You know, the outdoorsy type."

I looked at her dubiously. "Yeah, and knowing my luck, he'll smell like a bear and have the social graces of Freddy Krueger!" I said dryly, certain that this vacation was definitely going to be the worst ten days of my entire life!

Chapter Two

I *am lying on a white, sandy beach in my new mint-green bikini. Nearby is the beautiful blue ocean, splashing rhythmically against the shore. The bright sun overhead is tanning my body to a gorgeous bronze and my brown hair is magically becoming streaked with shades of shimmering gold. Surrounding me are the three most gorgeous guys I've ever seen in my life.*

"Come on Kate, please come dancing with me tonight," the blond lifeguard pleads.

"No Kate, don't go with him. I'll take you out to dinner at the most expensive restaurant in town," a dark-haired guy with broad shoulders promises me.

The third guy, a total fox with a surfboard, leans over me and my heart practically stops beating. I know he's going to say something wonderfully romantic, and I hold my breath in anticipation as he leans closer and closer to me. . . .

"Oh kids, look at the deer!" Mom's excited voice penetrated my sleep-fogged brain, banishing the beautiful dream I had been enjoying. I squeezed my eyes tightly closed, willing my dream to continue. I couldn't believe it—this was the first time in my life three gorgeous hunks had fought over me and now I'd never get the chance to choose which one I wanted.

"Kate, honey, you really should sit up and look at the marvelous scenery," Mom said from the front seat of the car.

I sighed in defeat, knowing that my mom wouldn't be satisfied until I sat up and acted enthusiastic. I opened my eyes and found myself staring at my brother's foot, his big toe sticking out of a hole in the end of his sock. Uttering a strangled gasp of disgust, I shoved his foot out of my face. Jeff was sound asleep, but as his foot hit the floor of the car, he mumbled something that sounded like "peanut butter" and changed his sleeping position.

I sat up straighter and rubbed the last of the sleep from my eyes. When we had left the house much earlier, it was still dark, but now the sun was high in the sky and I guessed it was around ten o'clock. I looked out the car window, immediately bored by the scenery my mom found so fascinating. We were on a two-lane highway, with thick woods on either side.

"Well, I see Sleeping Beauty has awakened." Dad grinned at me through his rear-view mirror. "Now, if we can wake up Prince Charming, we'll stop at a restaurant and get some breakfast."

I nudged my brother. "Time to eat," I whispered, giggling as his eyes immediately flew open and he sat up, instantly alert. I know my brother pretty well, and food is at the top of his list of priorities.

Jeff and I are pretty close, considering we're brother and sister. At least he doesn't treat me like a kid sister most of the time, and it's kind of flattering that most of the girls at school consider Jeff a major catch. I'm the first to admit that Jeff's fairly good-looking. He has nice sandy-brown hair and brown eyes and he's tall with an athletic build.

Still, I see Jeff in the mornings when he first gets out of bed, with his hair sticking out in a million directions and his face creased from the pillow. It always tickles me to see some girl flirting with him, and I wonder if she'd still be excited if she saw him brushing his teeth with toothpaste running down his chin.

"How much farther is it to the lake?" I asked, wishing we were in an airplane winging our way to California.

"We're about an hour and a half away from

the lake. If we want, we could just wait until we get to the cabin to eat breakfast," Dad said.

"No!" my mom and Jeff called out simultaneously.

"I don't want to wait a whole hour and a half to eat breakfast," Jeff exclaimed. "I'm a growing boy!" He looked at me, his brown eyes teasing me as they always did when he was about to say something rotten. "And Kate looks almost sickly. Oh, sorry, I made a mistake, that's just the way she always looks."

I elbowed him in the side. "Why don't you put your shoes on before I tell Susie that your feet smell like liver and onions!" I retorted, knowing that he wouldn't want Susie, his "true love," to hear about what stinky feet he had. Quick as a flash he grabbed me around the waist and started tickling me. "Stop!" I yelled, giggling.

"Hey, knock it off," Mom complained as my arm caught her in the back of the head. "The car is too small and you two are too big for this sort of roughhousing!"

"Come on, knock it off, little sister," Jeff said innocently. "Quit bothering me!" He still had his arms around me, driving me crazy as he tickled my ribs.

"Mom, make him stop!" I gasped, trying to wiggle away from him.

"Okay, okay!" Jeff laughed and released me.

"You're nothing but a big bully, Jeff Weatherby," I muttered, trying to catch my breath. "If you had to battle me by wits, I'd win hands down!"

Jeff laughed again. He leaned over and affectionately tousled my brown hair. "You're all right for a kid sister!" He grinned at me.

"Gee, I'm so glad you approve of me, considering you're stuck with me as your sister for the rest of your life!" I replied dryly.

"Hey Mom, is it possible to get a sister transplant?" Jeff asked. Once again the mischievous look crept into his eyes.

"Why don't you try a brain transplant!" I suggested.

"I hope you two can act civilized inside," Mom said as Dad pulled up in front of a restaurant.

Jeff and I looked at each other with very uncivilized faces, then dissolved into laughter.

"Well, here it is, everyone!" Dad said as we drove over a hill.

"Oh, isn't it beautiful," Mom gasped appreciatively.

I had to agree. Lake Vallecito was at the bottom of a valley surrounded on all sides by mountains and huge pine trees, just as Mom had described. The lake itself was a brilliant blue, the trees a deep green, and the distant mountains were topped with snow. *At least I'm going to spend the next ten days bored to death in beautiful surroundings*, I thought to myself.

We followed a winding road that led to the lake, then followed signs that pointed the way to Hidden Ranch.

"Boy, they weren't kidding when they named this place Hidden Ranch," I observed as our car turned down a narrow dirt road.

"Look, Jim, there's the Double O Saloon," Mom exclaimed, pointing to a large building that was constructed to resemble an old-fashioned saloon. "Your dad and I went there years ago when we first came here. They've got a huge dance floor and play great country and western music."

"Country and western!" Jeff made a gagging noise.

"Your cheatin' heart," I twanged in a nasal voice, giggling as Jeff joined in.

"You kids have no appreciation for good music," Mom interrupted our chorus.

"If country and western was good music, we'd appreciate it, right, Kate?" Jeff grinned.

"Right, but who wants to listen to a bunch of people singing through their noses about truck stops and lost love," I replied.

"Well, at least you can understand the words to country songs," Dad retorted.

"If it's a bar, it doesn't matter what kind of music they play. We're too young to go in anyway," I said, trying to end the discussion.

Mom shook her head. "It's not really a bar.

It's more of a hangout for all the tourists in the area. Kids of all ages are welcome inside."

Dad pulled to a halt in front of a small building that looked like a log cabin. "Here it is—home for the next ten days," he said. There was a sign on the door that said "Office."

"Where are the cabins?" I asked curiously, unable to see anything but woods and pine trees in the area.

"They're all spread out in the woods," Mom answered. "The trees thin out farther down the road. That's where you'll find the stables."

"*Stables*?" I practically squealed in surprise. "You mean there are horses I can ride? You never said anything about that before we left!"

"I didn't?" Mom laughed and smiled at me. "I guess it just slipped my mind. They also have hayrides and trail rides and all sorts of fun things."

"Mom! You never told me they had all that here!" I exclaimed, for the first time feeling a little bit excited about the vacation. For as long as I could remember, I'd wanted to take riding lessons, but we'd never been able to afford them. *Here's my chance to learn how to ride*, I thought, growing more excited by the minute.

"I'll go check us in and get the keys to our cabin," Dad said, opening his car door. He looked back at Jeff. "You want to come in with me? If I remember right, they have some fine taxidermy on the walls in the office."

"Sure," Jeff agreed. He and Dad disappeared into the office.

"Is there anything else you forgot to mention to me about this place?" I asked Mom curiously.

Mom thought for a moment. "Did I tell you they rent rowboats? Your dad and I have rented one for the whole ten days. He's hoping to get out in the middle of the lake and catch a record trout."

I nodded, not the least bit interested in this piece of news. I think fishing is the most boring sport in the whole world. I saw a wall plaque once that showed a fisherman in a rowboat that read: Fishing is a jerk on one end of the line waiting for a jerk on the other end. That saying pretty well sums up my feelings about fishing.

"They also have paddleboats you can rent," Mom added as an afterthought.

"Paddleboats?" I looked at her curiously. "What is a paddleboat?"

"You know, those little boats where you sit in a chair and there are bicycle pedals you push to move the boat through the water," Mom explained.

"They sound like fun," I said. *Maybe this vacation won't be so bad after all*, I thought to myself. *With horseback riding and paddleboats, at least I'll have something to do for the next ten days besides reading* Seventeen. *It's a shame that I'll only have my brother to do things with, though. Not that I mind spending time with Jeff, but it would be nice if I could do all these things with a boyfriend. Somehow I think things would seem even more interesting that way.*

"We're all checked in," Dad said, opening the car door and sliding in behind the steering wheel. "We're in cabin eight, which is down near the stables."

"You should have seen all the junk in the office, Kate," Jeff said to me. "They have stuffed trout and bass and all kinds of fish, a moose head with antlers, and a big bear."

"That's okay, just as long as you didn't see any human heads stuffed and hanging on the walls!" I kidded.

Jeff grinned at me and gave an evil laugh. "They're in the back room."

"Very funny, Jeff," I replied, suddenly thinking of something he'd said a few moments ago. "Did you say there was a stuffed bear in there?" Jeff nodded. "Dad, are there bears around here?" I asked worriedly.

"Oh, not too many," he answered nonchalantly.

"Not too many!" I squeaked. "*One* is too many!" Then I saw his twinkling eyes in the rearview mirror.

He laughed. "No, Kate, you don't have to worry about bears."

"The only wild animal you'll have to worry

about is your brother if he isn't fed three square meals a day," Mom said, making us all laugh.

"Let's go find our cabin," Dad said, starting up the car and moving down a small dirt road not much bigger than a path. "There it is," Dad said after a few minutes. He pointed to the rustic-looking cabin half hidden in the trees.

"And there's the stables," I exclaimed in delight, noticing how close our cabin was to the low, flat building that housed the horses.

"And there's the lake!" Jeff pointed to the other side of our cabin, where the sun deck jutted out just a stone's throw away from the edge of the lake water.

"Well, let's get the car unloaded," Mom said as Dad pulled our car as close to the cabin as he could get it. We'd still have to carry everything from the car about two hundred yards to the cabin.

"This is the worst part about going on vacation," I grumbled as Dad loaded my arms with suitcases from the trunk.

Dad laughed good-naturedly. "If we all pitch in, we'll be unloaded in no time at all," he said. "And once we're unloaded we can start having fun!"

"I feel like a pack mule," I said as Dad hung a satchel around my neck and handed me two suitcases to carry.

"You look like one, too." Jeff grinned.

"Ha-ha, very funny!" I stuck out my tongue at him, then started walking toward the cabin. When I was halfway there, I stopped and sat the suitcases down on either side of me. "Mom must have packed bricks in here," I mumbled, rubbing my hands together. Before I could grab the handles of the suitcases, a loud snort and a whinny drew my attention to the thickly wooded area on one side of the cabin.

I stared for a moment, unable to believe my eyes. At the edge of the woods was a guy on a horse. The horse was a beautiful black one, standing tall and majestic. But it was the guy on the horse's back who held my attention. This was no ordinary guy—he was straight out of one of my fantasies. My California surfer was right here at Lake Vallecito.

He didn't see me; instead he seemed to be looking beyond me toward the stables. I stared at him with interest. It was hard to tell how tall he was, since he was sitting on the back of a horse. But I could see how broad his shoulders were beneath the pale blue shirt he had on. The sunlight danced on his white-blond hair, while also emphasizing his deep, dark tan. He sat on the horse with an ease that I immediately envied. He looked like he belonged on the back of the horse!

My heart began thudding loudly as he turned his head in my direction, and for a split second our eyes met. Even from this distance, I was certain I could see the brilliant blue of his eyes. As I watched wordlessly, he suddenly tugged at the reins of the horse. The horse reared up on his hind legs and took off into the woods, disappearing from my sight. For a moment I just stood there, wondering if maybe I had just imagined the whole thing. But I knew I hadn't. The dream guy on the horse was real, and I thought he just might be the hunk to salvage my vacation.

Chapter Three

"I think I've got something!" Mom exclaimed, the tip of her fishing pole bending over the side of the rowboat.

"Set the hook!" Dad yelled eagerly, like he really wished the fish was on his pole instead of Mom's.

"How do you set the hook?" Mom squealed as the pole jerked in her hands. "Oh . . . I think I lost it." Her grin disappeared as her fishing line went slack.

"We've been out here for two hours and the most exciting thing that's happened so far is that Mom just lost a fish," I noted ruefully.

"I'll admit, the fishing has been a little slow this morning," Dad said.

"I told you when you got us all up at five o'clock this morning that all the fish would still be asleep," I replied, wishing I was anyplace but in the middle of this lake.

"Look at it this way,"Jeff said lazily. "If we

don't catch any fish, at least we've gotten lots of sun."

"Hmmm . . ." I mumbled, unconvinced. Jeff can be a little too darn optimistic at times. I hadn't exactly been thrilled when Dad got us all up this morning before dawn for some fishing. I normally don't mind family togetherness, but I definitely don't like it cramped in a tiny rowboat!

As Mom, Dad, and Jeff settled down to watch for fish, I found myself scanning the shoreline, hoping to catch a glimpse of the guy I'd seen the day before when we first arrived. *I wonder if I'll see him today*, I thought to myself. I tuned out the conversation going on around me and leaned back and closed my eyes.

I'm walking along the shore of the lake wearing Marcia's cute blue sundress. (In my fantasy I brought the dress with me.) It's sunset and the horizon is streaked with shades of pink and red. There is a small breeze that makes my skirt dance around my knees. Suddenly, in the distance I hear the sound of galloping horse hooves. I slowly turn around, and coming toward me is the boy on horseback. . . .

"I think I've got another one!" Mom's excited yell interrupted my daydream.

I put my fingers in my ears and squeezed my eyes more tightly closed. Now, where was I? Oh yeah, the guy on the horse. *He's gallop-*

ing toward me and he reins in, stopping his horse right in front of me. "I saw you from up the shore and I just had to come over and see who the beautiful girl was . . . all alone," he says to me in a deep, dreamy voice as he dismounts his horse.

"My name is Kate Weatherby," I say softly so he will have to lean closer to hear me.

"Kate—that's a lovely name." He smiles at me, a smile that could melt the soles off my shoes. "My name is. . . ."

I tried to think of a good name. I finally decided his name could be Stephen. Stephen is the name of my favorite soap opera star.

"My name is Stephen," he tells me, "and I think you're the girl I've been waiting for all my life." He looks at me, his eyes gazing intently into mine. He jumps back on his horse and holds his hand out to me. I take his hand, thrilled as he sweeps me up onto his horse with him and his strong arms enfold me. That's the way it always happens in the books I read, anyway.

I opened my eyes as Dad gave a triumphant yell and reeled in a nice-sized trout. *Oh great,* I thought, realizing that Dad's catch meant we'd be out here for another couple of hours.

I looked over the side of the boat, surprised to see that the water was so clear I could see my reflection perfectly. From what I'd learned in Earth Science, I'd expected the water to be murky with algae. I leaned over the side of the boat to get a better view of myself. My eyes are a nice shade of green, although my mouth is a little too wide to be perfect. As my reflection rippled slightly, I caught sight of what might be a pimple on the end of my chin. *It can't be*! I thought in dismay, leaning farther over for a closer look. The minute I leaned over, I knew I had made a major mistake. The boat rocked precariously and I felt myself toppling headfirst over the side.

Before I even had a chance to scream, I felt a hand grab me by the back of the neck as if I were a little puppy, and I was yanked back into the boat.

"Kate, it's easier to catch fish with a pole than jumping overboard to catch them in your hands," Jeff said, laughing.

I smiled at him gratefully, not even caring that he was teasing me as usual.

"I thought maybe you were so desperate to get off the boat, you were planning on swimming to shore." Dad grinned at me. "But I'm sure if we stay out here just a little while longer we'll have enough fish to fry for supper!"

I groaned inwardly at his words and leaned back a safe distance from the edge before closing my eyes. At least I could daydream to help pass the time!

I awoke early the next morning, ready for a little exploring. I dressed in record time, then went into the kitchen area, where Jeff was still asleep. I shook his shoulder lightly. "Jeff . . . wake up!"

He pulled the sheet up tighter around his neck and stopped snoring for a moment, but he didn't wake up.

"Hey, Jeff." I nudged him harder, and he cracked an eye open and looked at me. "Do you want to come exploring with me?" I asked brightly.

"What time is it?" he croaked, closing his eye again.

"Eight o'clock—time to rise and shine!"

Jeff sat up and looked at me in disbelief. "You woke me up at eight o'clock in the morning on vacation—when I could be sleeping late!" That gleam I knew so well sprang into his brown eyes. "Do you know what happens to girls who wake up their older brothers?"

"No, what?" I giggled, backing away from him.

"*This*!" Jeff yelled, springing up from the bed and advancing on me with his pillow held high over his head.

"Jeff . . . don't . . ." I tried to sound stern, but I laughed despite myself. "You'll wake up Mom and Dad," I warned.

"Mom and Dad left hours ago to go out on the boat," Jeff answered with a wicked grin. "And that leaves you totally at my mercy!" He started to chase me, swatting at me with his pillow.

I screamed and ran, then laughed wildly as

Jeff tripped over the leg of the table and went sprawling onto the floor. "See, you've been punished for trying to be mean to your poor little sister." I leaned against the doorway as he picked himself up off the floor, rubbing a reddened knee.

"So, do you want to come exploring with me or not?" I asked again.

"I think I'll tend to my wounds, then get me some breakfast," Jeff said.

I laughed. "Okay, I'll be back later," I told him, heading for the door.

"Have fun," Jeff said, then added with a grin, "and watch out for bears!"

I waved at him, then set off, anxious to explore the place where I was going to be spending the next nine days of my life. Ha, who was I kidding? I wanted to find that boy on the big black horse!

I started my search at the side of our cabin where I'd first seen him. There I found a well-worn path that led through the woods. I'm no Davy Crockett, or anything like that, but I figured I could handle a well-worn path with no problems.

"Okay, which way would Daniel Boone go?" I said aloud as I came to a fork in the path. I decided to go left, because I'm left-handed. I often make my decisions based on seemingly inconsequential stuff like that. It drives a lot of my friends crazy, but Marcia understands me perfectly. She makes her important decisions the same way. Marcia decided to take French last year because she needed a subject that started with the letter F. She'd chosen all her classes to go in alphabetical order: Algebra, Business Typing, Computer Workshop, Modern Dance, English, and French. She'd have taken Football if that had been the only class available that began with an F.

"Boy, I've only been gone one day and I already miss Marcia," I said aloud to keep myself company as I stepped over a fallen tree trunk in the path. "I wish she was here so I'd have somebody to talk to!"

I walked for about half an hour, then suddenly realized I was going in a direction that was taking me farther away from the stables. The stables—mentally I kicked myself. I should have gone to the stables first. After all, the guy had been on a horse!

I turned around and went back the way I'd come, frowning as I came to a clear, gurgling stream. *I didn't cross this before*, I thought, looking around in bewilderment. Around me were trees, and each tree looked exactly the same. I didn't know how I'd gotten off the path I'd been on, but it was obvious that I had, because nothing looked the least bit familiar. "Don't panic," I told myself calmly.

I looked at the sun, trying to figure out in what direction I was headed. But the trees were so close together and so tall, I couldn't see the sun at all. I crossed over the creek and continued following the path, certain that eventually I'd come out somewhere near our cabin. After another half hour of walking, I once again came to the creek and realized I'd somehow managed to walk in a huge circle. I was back in the same place where I had started! *I could be lost in these woods forever*, I thought, feeling panic rising up in my throat. I started walking faster, following a new path I'd found. I'd read lots of newspaper articles about people getting lost and never being seen again.

No, my mind tried to reason. *I'd be missed. Someone would come after me. I couldn't get lost in the woods. I was too young. I had too many things to do. . . . But worst of all, I'd never been in love*!

By this time I was running through the woods, thorns and branches scratching my face and arms. Wild thoughts were running through my mind. *I was too young to die without one last chocolate cupcake! I was too young to get eaten by wild animals. . . .*

My heart practically burst out of my chest at the thought of wild animals and bears. I've had an unreasonable fear of bears ever since I saw a movie called *The Night of the Grizzly*. For months afterwards I'd had nightmares about bears, and had seen bears in every shadow.

I sobbed a sigh of relief, seeing a break in the woods ahead. My eyes focused on the rays of sunshine coming through the opening in the dense brush as I ran toward it. As I plunged through the hole in the brush, I was certain that a dozen big, hungry bears were three feet behind me. Almost through the opening, I felt my foot catch on something. *It's a bear,* I thought wildly. *A bear's got my foot!* I screamed and tumbled to the ground, turning one complete somersault before landing on the ground with my nose pressed against the sweet-smelling earth. As I hit the ground, face down, the breath in my lungs escaped painfully.

"Who's that?" I heard a voice speaking from somewhere above me.

"I don't know, I've never seen her before," another voice said. "Is she all right?"

I slowly rolled over and my eyes widened in surprise. Standing over me were four girls and three boys, all about my age.

"That's my sister," a familiar voice said.

I sat up and took a deep breath, spotting Jeff standing nearby. *What a creep,* I thought, glaring at him irritably. While I was scared half to death, facing peril in the woods, he was hanging out with the only bunch of kids within a twenty-mile radius of the cabin! And who were these kids? Where had they come from? And how had Jeff found them without me?

My face flushed hotly as I realized what a fool I'd made of myself, bursting through the trees, screaming as if a bear actually was after me. Thank goodness my dream guy wasn't among the kids who'd seen me fall.

"Let me guess." A girl with dark hair and brown eyes smiled at me. "You thought you'd do a little exploring and you got hopelessly lost." She held out her hand to help me up.

I looked at her gratefully. "How'd you guess?" I grabbed her hand and pulled myself off the ground, quickly dusting myself off and running a hand through my hair, which was a tangle of twigs and thorns.

She laughed, and gestured toward the other kids. "I think all of us have gotten lost in the woods at least once." She smiled. "I'm Julie Harrison. Jeff said you're his sister, but we don't know your name."

"Oh, I'm Kate Weatherby," I replied, my face flushing once again.

"Hi, Kate. Welcome to Hidden Ranch!" Julie exclaimed, and all the other kids echoed her greeting. "You definitely know how to make a dramatic entrance!"

"Thanks." I grinned at Julie, wondering if she knew just how panicky I'd felt, lost in the woods. My grin widened as I looked at Julie and the other kids. *It will be so nice to hang out with a bunch of kids my age,* I thought. *And maybe they'll even know my dream guy!*

Chapter Four

"So is this your first time at Hidden Ranch?" Julie asked me as we all walked toward the stable building. I wasn't sure where we were going or why, but I wasn't about to lose this opportunity to talk to real teenagers instead of my parents or the fish in the lake.

"Yeah, and I have to admit, I wasn't too excited about coming here," I said truthfully, then hurriedly added, "but now that I see there are other people under the age of forty, I'm sure it will be fun."

"I felt the same way the first time my family came to Hidden Ranch. I wondered what I was going to do for two whole weeks stuck in the middle of nowhere!" Julie exclaimed, smiling up at Jeff as he fell in step with the two of us.

"You should have heard Kate carrying on about coming here, and we're only going to be here for ten days," Jeff said, and I was shocked to see him give Julie a goofy smile. He smiled that way every time he was around Nanette Withers, the head cheerleader at our high school. I looked at Julie with renewed interest. If my brother liked her, we'd probably be spending a lot of time with her.

"There's a bunch of us whose families come here every year. We call ourselves the KFF," Julie explained with a grin. "Kids of Fishing Freaks!" She had really cute dimples.

"Where are you from?" I asked curiously.

"Kansas City, Missouri. My parents have been flying out here every year for the past three years to fish." She pointed to the rest of the kids walking just ahead of us. "We're a pretty diverse bunch. Sam is fifteen and he's from New Mexico. Johnny is sixteen and from Oklahoma." I inspected the two boys. Both were dark-haired and sort of cute, but neither was anywhere near as interesting as the blond boy I'd seen the day before. "Martha and Mary are sixteen and seventeen, sisters from Nevada. And Christy is fourteen and she's from Kansas," Julie finished.

"What about you? How old are you?" Jeff asked, the dopey grin still pasted to his face.

"Seventeen. I'm going to be a senior next year," she answered.

"Me, too," Jeff replied. They looked at each other with pleased expressions, like they'd just discovered they'd both won the state lottery.

"So, this is the whole gang, huh?" I asked, feeling slightly let down. Apparently the blond guy wasn't a regular around here.

"That's the gang—oh, except for Stony," Julie replied.

My heart began to beat rapidly. Stony . . . he had to be the guy on the horse, he just *had* to be! Stony was a perfect name for a dream guy. It sounded so cool! I listened avidly as Julie continued. "Stony isn't actually in the KFF club. He works here at Hidden Ranch every summer. That's what we're doing here," she said as we stopped at the fence that surrounded the stable area. Sam and Johnny disappeared into the stables. "They want to see what time Stony gets off work today," she explained.

"Uh . . . does Stony have blond hair?" I asked, trying to sound nonchalant.

"Yeah, why?" Julie turned and looked at me curiously.

"I think I might have caught a glimpse of him yesterday," I answered, fighting the impulse to run my hand through my hair. It was just my luck that I'd probably meet him now, with my hair standing on end, full of brambles and broken twigs.

"If you caught a glimpse of Stony, you'd remember him," Julie remarked dryly, then smiled up at Jeff. "So, what classes are you going to take for your senior year?"

As Jeff and Julie talked, I turned my attention back to the stable door, my heart beating wildly in anticipation. I knew it was sort of silly for me to be so excited about a guy I'd never even met before and had only seen once, but I couldn't help it.

"He's not here," Sam said as he and Johnny came back to the fence where the rest of us were waiting.

"Why don't we go on down to the beach?" Martha suggested. "Stony will know where to find us when he gets off work."

Sam looked at his watch. "It's almost eleven o'clock now. Why don't we meet back here at noon? That will give us all time to eat lunch, then we can go down to the beach and swim for a couple of hours."

"What cabin are you guys in?" Julie asked Jeff as everyone began to go separate ways.

"Number eight, over there." He pointed in the direction of our cabin.

"I'm in number three, over that way." Julie pointed in the opposite direction.

"Where is the beach?" I asked curiously.

"Down the road about a mile," Julie answered. "It's not really an official beach. It's just an area of shoreline that's pretty clear of brush and the lake bottom slopes gently. We've sort of adopted it as our private beach. You guys are going to come swimming with us, aren't you?" She looked at both of us, but I knew she was really talking to Jeff. I didn't have to be a brilliant detective to tell that they were definitely attracted to each other.

Jeff looked over at me and nodded. "Sure, it sounds like fun."

"Great!" Julie smiled at him. "We'll meet you back here in about an hour." She waved and started walking toward her cabin.

"They all seem really nice, don't they?" I said as Jeff and I began walking back to our cabin.

"Yeah, they do. It'll be fun having a bunch of kids to hang out with," Jeff said with a small smile.

"And Julie's really pretty," I added slyly, glancing at him quickly to catch his reaction.

"She's all right," he replied nonchalantly.

"All right!" I hooted with laughter. "If you'd smiled at her any longer, your lips would have fallen right off your face!"

"Don't be a jerk." Jeff scowled at me, and I noticed the tips of his ears were turning a bright red, a sure sign that he was embarrassed.

"I wonder what Susie would think of Julie?" I grinned as Jeff's face turned beet-red. "She'd probably be real upset to know her steady guy is making goo-goo eyes at another girl."

"I wasn't making goo-goo eyes," Jeff protested. "And blackmail is against the law."

"Who's talking about blackmail?" I asked innocently.

"Besides," Jeff said more assuredly. "I haven't done anything that you can tell Susie about."

"Not yet . . . but we still have nine whole days left of this vacation," I reminded him.

"Don't remind me," Jeff replied. "I just hope Susie doesn't find anyone else while I'm gone."

I looked at my brother in surprise. I didn't know guys worried about things like that. "She wouldn't dare," I said sympathetically. "I'm sure she knows you're the best thing that's ever happened to her."

Jeff looked at me in surprise, then threw his arm around my shoulders. "Come on, let's go get something to eat!" he said, and together we made our way back to our cabin.

Mom and Dad were back from fishing when we returned to the cabin. "Here's our explorers," Dad said as Jeff and I came into the kitchen. "Did you find anything of interest?" he asked.

"Jeff found a new girlfriend," I teased him.

"And Kate got lost in the woods and thought she was going to be eaten by bears," Jeff returned. I flushed with embarrassment, remembering how I'd fallen to the ground almost on top of the gang of kids.

"Did you catch any fish?" I asked, changing the subject quickly.

"Enough for a big pan of fried fish for supper tonight," Dad replied proudly. "Your mother even caught a trout big enough to keep."

Mom smiled with pleasure, removing the coffeepot from the stove top. "And your father promised me that if I cook up the mess of fish he caught for supper tonight, then tomorrow night he'll take us all out to dinner." She poured two cups of coffee, then sat down at the small dinette table.

"What's for lunch?" Jeff asked, opening the refrigerator door and rummaging through the contents.

"There's all kinds of luncheon meats in there for sandwiches," Mom replied. "What have you two got planned for this afternoon?"

"We're meeting a bunch of kids down by the stables, then we're going swimming in the lake," Jeff answered, pulling out packages of bologna and cheese.

"That sounds like fun," Mom replied, sipping her coffee and frowning slightly. "Is there a lifeguard at the lake?" She looked at my dad worriedly.

"Ah, Mom, you worry too much," Jeff protested.

"I'm sure they'll be fine," Dad assured Mom. "If they're all going together, they'll be okay. Just keep an eye on each other."

"You don't have to worry about me," I said. "I wouldn't swim in a place where there's no clean concrete bottom to put my feet on." I shuddered at the very thought. "I'm just going to sunbathe and concentrate on getting a tan."

"And you know I'm an excellent swimmer," Jeff reminded Mom, talking around a big bite of his sandwich.

"What time are you going?" Mom asked.

Jeff looked down at his watch. "In about half an hour," he replied.

"Half an hour!" I squealed, thinking of all the things I needed to do before we left. "I've got to change clothes, fix my hair, and put on makeup!" I headed for my bedroom.

"For crying out loud, Kate, we're just going swimming," Jeff called after me.

You may be going swimming, but I'm going to see my dream guy, I thought to myself as I hurried into my room and shut the door behind me.

Thirty minutes later Jeff and I made our way back to the stables, where several of the other kids were already waiting.

"Hi." Martha greeted us with a friendly smile. She and her sister Mary looked enough alike to be twins. Both were slightly chubby, with brown hair, brown eyes, and warm smiles that made you want to smile back.

"Hi," I answered.

"You look a little better than you did earlier," Martha observed with a little giggle.

"Thanks, I feel better now that I brushed all the brambles out of my hair," I smiled ruefully. I was appalled when I looked in the mirror in my room. My hair had been full of twigs, my face had been streaked with dirt, and I had torn the T-shirt I was wearing. In my mad dash through the woods, the woods had definitely won! I felt better now, wearing my new mint-green bikini with a matching cover-up, and with my face freshly scrubbed and made up.

"Mary and I got lost in the woods two years ago, and I can still remember how scary it was. We were lost until after dark."

"What happened?" I asked, shivering as I thought about being lost in those woods at night.

Martha giggled once again. "We started arguing about what we should do. I wanted to stay where we were and wait for somebody to find us and Mary wanted us to keep walking until we found our way out. We were fighting so loud, the search party had no trouble finding us." Her grin widened. "My mom said it was the one time she was glad that both Mary and I have big mouths and fight all the time. Hey, here comes Julie and Johnny; that's everybody."

"Let's go!" Johnny yelled to everyone, and we all took off down the road that led past the stables.

"It looks like a case of summer love brewing," Martha said, turning around and looking at Jeff and Julie, who were lagging behind the rest of the group.

"I don't know about that—Jeff has a steady girlfriend back home," I replied.

"Your brother is cute," Martha said with another of her giggles. Then she sighed. "But Julie always gets the cute guys."

"Do a lot of cute guys come here during the summer?" I asked, as always passionately interested in the subject of cute guys.

"Oh, loads," Martha answered. "But a lot of them are only interested in the fishing, and others like your brother have girlfriends back home. The rest of them are usually one-timers—they come here once and they never come back." She smiled at me. "Personally, I don't believe in summer love; it's just too hard to maintain when the summer is over."

I didn't say anything in return. What could I say? I'm not exactly an expert on summer love—or any other kind of love, for that matter!

We walked along the road for about half a mile, then cut off onto a small path. This time, walking in the woods wasn't so frightening; in fact, it was fun. Sam acted like he was Tarzan and kept trying to get Johnny to act like a monkey. Their antics entertained us for the remainder of the walk.

We left the path and entered a clearing, and there we were at the beach. The beach area was just like Julie had described it. There was no sand, no lifeguards, but there was a wide expanse of shoreline that sloped gently into the water. There was also enough of a clearing for a volleyball net that was stretched parallel to the water, with enough room for blankets and beach towels. We stretched out our towels, and within minutes, all the guys, along with Julie and Christy, had hit the water.

"Aren't you going to swim?" Martha asked me, pulling off her T-shirt and adjusting her pink one-piece bathing suit.

I shook my head. "Not right now," I hedged, not willing to get into the lake along with the fish and other creepy crawlies that might be lurking there. "I think I'll do a little sunning first." I lay back on the blanket as she shrugged and ran toward the water. I propped my head up on my hand and watched the others splashing and yelling. Mary lay on a beach towel near me, looking like she had fallen asleep. The sun was hot, and high in the sky, and the water looked inviting, but I'd never liked the idea of swimming in a lake. Besides, I wanted my hair and makeup to stay nice just in case Stony showed up later. I lay on my back and closed my eyes against the sun, enjoying the feeling of warmth that was spreading through my body.

"Hi," came a deep voice right next to me.

I heard the voice as I awoke, surprised that I had fallen sound asleep. I groaned irritably, angry at being awakened, since I'd been dreaming about the guy on the horse. I opened my eyes groggily, ready to yell at whoever had pulled me from my dreams. My eyes flew wide open in shock. There, sitting on the edge of my beach towel, was the guy who had just played a starring role in my dream!

"Oh . . . uh . . . hi!" I sat up and pushed a strand of hair out of my eyes.

"Hi there. My name's Steve Mahoney," he said, holding out his hand to me. "But my friends call me Stony." He smiled as I placed my hand in his. "I have a feeling we are going to be good friends."

As he shook my hand, I stared at him like I was in a trance. He was the most gorgeous-looking guy I'd ever seen in my life! His hair was a pale white-blond that contrasted with his dark tan. His eyes were the purest blue I'd ever seen, and the cleft in his chin only added to his incredible good looks. *And his name is Steve*, I thought to myself in disbelief. *Just like my fantasy . . . it must be fate or destiny or something!*

"Are you going to tell me your name?" he asked, amusement shining from his gorgeous eyes as he released my hand.

"Oh . . . uh . . . I'm Kate Weatherby," I stuttered, flushing as I realized I'd been staring at him.

"Well, Kate Weatherby, where are you calling from?" he asked, moving closer to me. He smelled like fresh hay and horses and leather.

"I'm from Denver," I answered, hoping I didn't sound as breathless as I felt.

"Denver, huh? I'll have to visit there soon if they grow all the girls as pretty as you." He smiled at me again, and I felt a hot flush steal over me, from the tip of my head to my big toe.

This is a dream, I thought to myself. *I'm still asleep on the beach towel and this is part of the dream I've been having.* Still, everything seemed too vivid to be a dream. I was perfectly aware of the other kids yelling in the water, the sun beating down on me, the birds singing in the nearby trees, and a bee buzzing lazily around my head. No, this certainly wasn't a dream.

"Are you all right?" Stony asked, his smile turning to an expression of concern. "You look sort of dazed."

"Yeah, I'm fine. I guess I'm not awake yet."

"Oh, wow, I didn't know you were asleep. I didn't mean to wake you up," he exclaimed, tilting his head to one side and grinning at me crookedly.

"Oh no, it's fine. I wanted to wake up!" I smiled at him, still unable to believe that such a great-looking guy was sitting on the edge of my towel, talking to me.

"Hey, Stony!" Sam called from the water. "Come on in!" The others called out to us. "Come on, you two!"

Stony laughed and waved at them, then

stood up. "Come on, we're being paged." He pulled his T-shirt over his head, revealing a firmly muscled, bronzed chest. He threw the shirt over to one side and looked at me, with that crooked smile that just made him more devastatingly handsome. "Aren't you coming in?"

"Oh, I don't know," I said hesitantly, afraid to admit my fear of the slimy lake.

"Come on, the water always feels great at this time of day." He held out his hand to me. "Come on, Kate. Come swimming with me."

I looked at his hand stretched out to me, knowing I had two choices. I could sit there on the shore all alone and let Stony go in and have a good time with the other kids. Or I could face—with Stony—the prospect of the squishy, muddy bottom covered with creepy crawlies. Taking a deep breath, I reached up and grabbed his hand.

Chapter Five

I put my hand in his, hoping mine wasn't too moist. Sometimes I think that I'm the only girl in the whole world who worries about sweaty palms and bad breath and stuff like that.

Stony led me toward the water. When we got to the edge, I halted, eyeing the bright blue water suspiciously.

"You can swim, can't you?" Stony asked, his blue eyes making me feel weak in the knees.

"Of course," I replied with a small laugh, but I made no attempt to move closer to the water. "But I usually swim in swimming pools, with concrete bottoms and filter systems," I added truthfully, hoping he didn't think I was a big baby.

"This is pretty much the same thing," Stony said, and started to pull me into the water, but I dug in my heels, not giving an inch.

"What's the matter, Kate?" he asked with what appeared to be genuine concern.

"Uh . . . there are fish in that water. And what about leeches and turtles and stuff like that?" I knew I was being silly, but I couldn't help it. Knowing my luck, a turtle would bite off my big toe, or a fish would jump into my bikini bottom, or a leech would attach itself. . . .

Stony smiled patiently and dropped my hand. "Kate, there are no leeches in this water, and look at all the kids out there splashing and yelling. Believe me, when we all get in the water, the turtles and the fish go to another part of the lake!" He smiled gently. "But if you don't want to go in, that's okay. I'll sit and talk to you."

I shook my head, touched that he would forego the pleasure of swimming for me. "I'll go in. I'll just go in slow."

He held out his hand to me once again. "I promise you, Kate; I won't let anything happen to you." He grinned at me coaxingly, and I knew no matter how scared I was, no matter how squeamish I felt, I was going to go into that lake with Stony.

I felt my courage growing as Stony's hand enclosed mine. He smiled at me reassuringly and I let him lead me into the water.

I gasped as the cold water licked at my ankles and the mud on the bottom of the lake squished up between my toes. "It's so cold!" I exclaimed.

Stony laughed, exposing his straight, white teeth. "This lake is fed by a lot of fresh mountain springs. That's why it's exceptionally clear and clean. You'll get used to it." He squeezed my hand encouragingly. I wondered if the warmth I felt at being so close to him, combined with the cold water, would make steam shoot out of my ears.

I grinned gamely and allowed him to lead me deeper into the water. The rest of the kids gathered around us, laughing and teasing me.

"The water's nice once you get in," Christy called encouragingly.

"Don't be a chicken, Kate," Mary yelled.

"Don't call her a chicken," Martha said, glaring at her sister.

"Come on, Kate, the water's great!" Sam grinned at me, then dove beneath the surface of the water. He surfaced a few yards away, spitting water at Christy like a whale.

"Hey, stop it!" Christy protested, and dove after Sam, who cut through the water like an Olympic swimmer. I watched them chasing each other and laughing, envying their ease in the lake water.

Stony urged me forward another step, and now the water was up to my knees. "Thanks for being so patient with me." I smiled shyly at Stony. "I'm really a good swimmer, it's just that I've never been in a lake before."

"Oh, Stony always gives *special* attention to the new girls," Julie said from nearby. Then, with a flip of her wet hair, she swam off toward Jeff.

I looked at Stony curiously. Julie had sounded sort of funny, like she was mad or something because Stony was paying attention to me. Did she like Stony? If she did, why was she openly flirting with my brother?

Stony saw my look. "Don't pay any attention to her." And as he pulled me deeper into the water and closer to him, all thoughts of Julie fled from my mind.

Swimming in a lake isn't so bad, I thought, *especially with Stony right beside me.* I wanted to think that I was just naturally overcoming my fears and allowing my brave courage to shine through, but I knew I was overcoming my fear of the water because Stony was smiling at me and it was suddenly very important that I impress him!

After Stony led me into the water up to my waist, he released my hand and grinned at me. "I'll race you to where Sam is," he challenged.

I looked out to the place where Sam was treading water about a hundred yards away. "You're on!" I answered, and without thinking twice, I plunged beneath the water and began swimming for all I was worth. I'm a pretty good swimmer, but I quickly found out that Stony was much better. By the time I reached the spot where the race was to end, he was already there, treading water and grinning at me with that funny, crooked smile that made my heart beat faster. I noticed that his eyes were the exact same intense blue as the water we were in.

"I win," he exclaimed. "But you're a pretty good swimmer," he complimented me, pushing his wet hair off his forehead. He swam a few strokes away from me, then called over his shoulder, "I just hope the freshwater sharks don't bite you."

"Sharks!" I stared at him in horror, frantically treading water. I looked all around me, and was able to see the bottom of the lake through the clear, cold water. "Since when are there sharks in lakes?"

"They're great big fish that only bite pretty girls in green bikinis." He grinned widely, making the cleft in his chin deepen attractively.

I realized he was teasing me. "And what do girls in green bikinis have to do to protect themselves from these vicious freshwater sharks?"

"There's only one way you can save yourself. You have to agree to be my date tomorrow night at the cookout," he said.

A date! He was actually asking me for a date! I kept my expression blank, not wanting him to see just how excited I really was. "What cookout?" I asked nonchalantly.

"We're having a campfire tomorrow night

down by the stables," Stony explained. "We do it about once a week, and we always have a really good time," He paused a moment. "So, will you go with me?"

I pretended to think about it for a moment. "Is the bite of a lake shark deadly?" I asked, trying to suppress a smile.

"Oh, well . . . *why*?" Stony asked, narrowing his eyes.

"I was just trying to figure out which would be more painful, the bite of a freshwater shark or being your date for an evening." I grinned as Stony burst out laughing.

"I promise, I'll try to make our date as painless as possible," he said.

"Okay, then I guess we've got a date," I answered.

"Hey Stony, why don't you and Kate come in and we'll play some volleyball!" Johnny yelled from the shore.

Stony looked at me. "Are you up for volleyball?"

"Sure," I answered, grateful for anything that would get me out of the water. Although the water didn't bother me as much as I thought it would, I still wasn't thrilled about it.

Stony and I swam leisurely toward shore. As he moved a little bit ahead of me in the water, I noticed the way his back muscles rippled as he swam. He seemed so smooth and sure of himself. Oh, how I wished I could tell Marcia about Stony, and how I wished she was right here to see him. But I wished even harder that tomorrow night would hurry and get here!

Later that afternoon, I stood in the small gift section of the office, trying to choose a postcard to send Marcia. I had wanted to call her and tell her all about Stony and my afternoon with him, but Mom and Dad said it was too expensive. I finally decided on a scenic postcard that showed the lake at sunset.

"If you want to write on that right now, I'll send it first thing in the morning," the woman behind the cash register said to me as I pulled out a dollar to pay her.

"Terrific." I smiled, eager to have Marcia get the postcard. I took the pen the woman offered me and flipped the postcard over to the blank side.

Dear Marcia,

Having a wonderful time, glad you're not here. (Ha!) Actually, wish you were here to see the gorgeous hunk I've got a date with tomorrow night. Get this—his name is Stony. Actually, his name is Steve, and he's blond and beautiful! Gotta go—gory details will follow. . . .

Your best friend, XXXOOO

Kate

I giggled as I signed my name, knowing Marcia would go nuts waiting to hear more. I bought a stamp and attached it to the postcard, then handed it back to the cashier.

"Hey, Kate, what's going on?"

I turned to see Julie coming into the office.

"I just got a postcard to send my best friend back home," I explained. "What are you doing in here?" I asked.

"I was just walking by and saw you through the window." She walked outside the office with me. "So, what'd you think of our little gang of kids?"

I grinned. "They all seem really nice, and they're all so different!"

"Yeah, we're a pretty motley bunch." Julie smiled, and I noticed again what a great smile she had. I wasn't surprised to discover earlier that day that she was a cheerleader back home.

"I can't believe how funny Sam is," I said with a laugh, remembering how he had kept us laughing all afternoon.

"Yeah, Sam is really great," Julie agreed. "He's also an award-winning gymnast. Sometimes I think Sam would rather walk on his hands than his feet!"

"I definitely got that impression." I laughed, thinking about how Sam had tried to play volleyball by standing on his hands and returning the ball with his feet.

"Sam and Johnny are really good friends,"

Julie continued. "They met here one summer, but they write to each other all year long. Johnny is the sane one and Sam is crazy. They make a good pair."

"Christy seems pretty quiet," I observed.

Julie nodded in agreement. "I think it's because she's the youngest of the group. She's only fourteen and sort of insecure about it."

"Then there's Martha and Mary," I said, thinking of the two sisters. I'd really liked Martha, who'd been especially friendly to me that afternoon.

Julie laughed. "The only thing they agree on is disagreeing about everything! They're easygoing with everyone but each other." Julie grinned at me. "And that's everyone in our little group."

"Well, not everyone. What about Stony?" I asked, trying to sound nonchalant.

"Oh yeah, him." The smile faded from Julie's face as she shrugged her shoulders. "Stony is totally gorgeous. What else is there to say about him?"

Something about the way she said that convinced me that she really didn't want to talk about him. "Stony's not really one of us," she added.

"He seems really smooth," I said, remembering how pleased I'd been that Stony had stayed by my side all afternoon, although we really hadn't gotten a chance to talk to each other. It's kind of hard to talk in the middle of a volleyball game.

"Stony's smooth all right. Practice makes perfect." She looked down at her watch. "Oops, I've got to go. It's supper time." She waved to me. "See you tomorrow."

I watched her walk away, wondering what she'd meant by her last statement about Stony. Practice makes perfect . . . that didn't exactly sound like a compliment. Something about the way Julie talked about Stony bothered me, but I couldn't put my finger on what it was.

I shrugged my shoulders, dismissing it from my mind. What difference did it make? *I have a date with Stony tomorrow night, and that's what's important,* I thought as I began walking toward our cabin. I had only gone a little ways when I saw Jeff heading in my direction.

"Mom and Dad sent me on a search mission for you," he explained. "Supper is ready."

I nodded and fell into step beside him. "I had a great time today," I told Jeff as we headed back.

"Yeah, it was fun," he agreed. "And you did pretty well for your first time swimming in a lake."

"Thanks!" I smiled at him brightly. It was so rare that Jeff actually gave me a real compliment.

"Of course, it wouldn't have anything to do

with a certain blond guy, would it?" Jeff grinned at me slyly.

"Don't be ridiculous," I lied. "I would have gotten into the water whether Stony had been there or not."

"Yeah, sure." Jeff stared at me, apparently unconvinced. "I'll tell you one thing. If you smiled at Stony much longer, your lips would have fallen right off your face!" He grinned widely, obviously pleased that he'd been able to throw my words back in my face.

"I guess we'll both have to be careful," I said seriously.

"Careful about what?" Jeff asked curiously.

"Well, if we *both* aren't careful, we'll end up being known as the lipless wonders!" I grinned as my brother shook his head at me.

"Come on, I'll race you to the cabin." Before the words were even out of his mouth, Jeff had sprinted ahead.

"Jeff Weatherby, you always were a cheater!" I yelled, laughing as I ran after him.

Chapter Six

"Hey, Kate! Are you awake?"

Startled, I jumped at the loud whisper coming from just outside my window. I knew it was early, although I'd been awake for only a few minutes. I scrambled out of bed and went to the window to see Martha, her face pressed against the screen. "Oh good, you *are* awake. I didn't know if you were an early riser or a late sleeper."

I grinned at her and yawned loudly. "It depends what I do the night before. If I stay out late, I sometimes sleep until noon."

Martha nodded, then grinned. "Last night must have been pretty boring, right?"

"Right!" I laughed. "What time is it, anyway?"

"Seven-thirty," Martha replied.

"What are you doing up so early?" I asked.

"My parents and Mary left about a half hour ago to go fishing for the day and I got lonely," she explained. "Why don't you come on out and we can take a walk and figure out what we're going to do for the rest of the day."

"Okay," I agreed. "Give me a few minutes and I'll be right out." I moved over to the closet and quickly pulled on a pair of jeans and a sweatshirt. Although by afternoon it would be hot, the evenings and early mornings were quite cool.

I hurried quietly into the bathroom, washed my face and brushed my teeth, then tiptoed by my still-sleeping brother. Once again, my parents' room was empty, and I knew they were probably already out in the boat.

I stepped outside and breathed deeply, enjoying the fresh, strong pine scent in the air. It was a beautiful morning, and I wondered briefly if I would have found it as beautiful if I didn't have a date with Stony that evening.

"That was quick," Martha exclaimed, coming around the corner of the cabin and walking up on the sun deck to stand next to me.

"It's pretty out this morning, isn't it?" I said, looking out toward the distant snow-capped mountains.

Martha nodded. "Every morning is pretty here. Being at Lake Vallecito is sort of like walking into a picture postcard." She touched my arm lightly. "Come on, let's take a walk."

I looked at her dubiously, then grinned. "You aren't going to get us lost in the woods, are you?"

She laughed. "No, I promise we'll stay on the paths I know."

We walked down the stairs of the sun deck and started down the path I had taken the day before, when I got lost.

"I can't believe how many chipmunks there are around here," I commented as one of the furry creatures scampered by, pausing to look at us curiously.

"They're real tame, too," Martha said. "Watch this." She stopped and reached into her pocket and pulled out a handful of shelled peanuts. As I watched in amazement, Martha held one of the nuts out to the chipmunk, who approached her hand brazenly and took the nut from her before running off into the woods.

'Wow, that's amazing!" I exclaimed.

"Ah, that's nothing." Martha laughed and sat down on the ground. "Now watch." She took another peanut and placed it on top of her head, then sat very still. The chipmunk approached her once again. I could see his little nose wiggling and sniffing. Then suddenly he ran up Martha's arm and across her shoulders and reached up and grabbed the nut from the top of her head. He leapt off her head and ran off again.

"That is absolutely fantastic!" I exclaimed as Martha stood up and brushed off the seat of her jeans.

"They're all like that," Martha explained as we began walking again. "They're fed by all the tourists and the people who run the resort, and over the years they've become more like pets than wild animals."

"That's really neat," I said, thinking that I'd have to get some peanuts and show Jeff this trick. "How come you didn't go fishing with your parents and Mary this morning?" I asked as we walked leisurely along the path.

Martha grimaced. "I hate to fish." Her grimace turned to a scowl. "Mary hates to fish, too. She just went with Mom and Dad because she's trying to impress them. She wants a real expensive suede coat, so she's doing everything possible to get on their good side. It's sickening!"

I laughed. "I guess you don't want a suede coat," I said.

Martha shook her head. "No way—at least not enough to spend a whole day in a rowboat with my parents!" We came to a fork in the path and Martha gestured to the left. "I don't know where that path leads, so we should go this way. There's a really cool place up ahead I'll show you. I found it by accident last year. It's got a little waterfall and a pretty pool of spring water."

I nodded and fell into step behind her as the path narrowed.

"So, what do you think of us KFFers?" Martha asked, stepping over a fallen tree limb.

"Everyone seems really nice," I answered. "Sam is so funny. Johnny seems nice, and

Christy is really sweet. And I think my brother is getting hooked on Julie."

Martha laughed. "All the guys get hooked on Julie. She's the bubbly cute type guys go for."

"She seems nice," I said, since Martha's assessment of Julie seemed a bit negative.

"Yeah, Julie is all right. Although I know if we were going to the same high school, she wouldn't give me the time of day if we passed each other in the hall," Martha said.

"Why not?" I asked.

Martha looked at me over her shoulder. "Kate, think about it. Julie is a cheerleader at her school; she probably belongs to a real exclusive clique. Now look at me—I'm overweight and nowhere as good-looking as she is."

"That's not true," I protested. True, Martha was no beauty queen, but she had a great sense of humor and a really pretty smile.

She stopped and turned around to face me. "You don't have to be polite. I'm *not* very pretty, but it really doesn't bother me. Oh, there was a time when I wished things had turned out differently, but now I feel much better about myself."

I looked at her, slightly uncomfortable, unsure of what to say.

"I like myself, Kate," Martha continued. "True, I'll never be a raving beauty, but I'm smart, and I have a good sense of humor, and someday I'll find a guy who thinks I'm the most beautiful girl in the world. In the meantime, I'm happy being me."

I looked at her with admiration, and she smiled back at me. There are very few of my friends back home who really like themselves. Most of the time I think I'm okay, but there are times when I think I'm the dumbest, ugliest loser ever born.

"What about Stony? What do you think of him?" I asked, changing the subject to the one that was uppermost in my mind.

"Stony? Stony is great," Martha said, as she turned around and started to walk again.

I hurried after her, unwilling to miss a single word she said about Stony.

"In a lot of ways, Stony is sort of a loner," Martha explained as we began to climb a steep incline. "He hangs out with all of us, and he's about the nicest guy I've ever met, but he keeps his feelings to himself."

"Is there something going on between him and Julie?" I asked hesitantly.

"Stony and Julie? Not that I know of. Why?"

"Oh, I don't know. I just get a funny feeling when I see them together," I replied, remembering all the snide comments Julie had made about him.

Martha shrugged. "Not that I know of—and usually I make it my business to know everything that's going on around here," she added with a giggle.

"I'm going to the campfire cookout with him tonight," I confided, my excitement growing as I spoke the words aloud.

"You'll have a great time. Those cookouts are a lot of fun."

"I've always thought that sitting around a campfire with a group of people would be sort of fun," I said, thinking how romantic it would be to sit next to Stony in front of a campfire and watch the firelight play on his handsome features. Suddenly I giggled.

"What's so funny?" Martha asked, grunting as she crawled over a large rock.

"I was just remembering a date I had. I had a crush on a guy named Guy Williams, so one day I invited him over for a candlelight dinner." I stopped talking long enough to clamber over the rock. "Anyway, my mom was really cooperative about my dinner plans. She helped me cook a gourmet dinner and let me use her very best china. The table looked beautiful, and when Guy arrived he was dressed for the occasion in a dark blue suit. Anyway, when we sat down at the table, I started to light the candles, and somehow the curtains in the dining room got in the way and they caught on fire."

"Oh no! What happened then?" Martha turned around and shot me a look of horror.

I giggled at the memory. "I started yelling and Guy threw his glass of water on the fire to put it out." I grinned ruefully. "It took me two months' worth of allowance to pay my parents for the ruined curtains, but the worst part was Guy went back to school and told everyone what a 'hot' date he'd had with me! Anyway, after that little incident, I don't think candlelight is so romantic anymore." I paused as I heard a dull roaring noise. "What's that?"

"Come on," Martha called back to me, and began to walk faster. I hurried after her, catching my breath as we came into a small clearing: A small but powerful waterfall was rushing down into a pool of the clearest water I'd ever seen.

"This place is beautiful!" I breathed almost reverently. I walked over to the edge of the pool and peered in, surprised that the water was so shallow and the bottom was clearly visible. "Have you ever swum in it?" I asked.

Martha shook her head. "The water is freezing! Besides, the owner of the resort told me this pool can be deceiving. It looks like it's only three feet deep, but actually it's almost twelve feet deep."

"Wow, the water is so crystal clear!" I exclaimed.

"It's mountain spring water," Martha explained as she sat down on a large flat rock near the edge of the water.

"I can't believe how much I would have missed if we hadn't come to Lake Vallecito," I said thoughtfully, joining her on the rock. "I had no idea it was so beautiful up here." But my thoughts were also on Stony. *I can't wait until tonight*, I thought to myself. In less than twelve hours I'd be on a date with Stony. Even though I was having fun with Martha, this was probably going to be the longest day of my life!

I stood in front of the bathroom mirror and looked at my reflection. I smiled with satisfaction. "This is about as good as you get," I said to my reflection. My brown hair was clean and shining, framing my face in soft curls. My makeup was light and natural-looking, subtly emphasizing my green eyes. I was dressed in a pair of jeans and a cotton green-and-pink sweater. Martha had told me that everyone dressed casually for the cookouts.

"Kate, would you hurry up? I've got to shave," Jeff protested, banging on the bathroom door.

"Don't worry, Julie won't notice the three whiskers growing on your chin." I giggled, picking up my perfume and spraying myself from head to toe.

"Very funny," Jeff said dryly through the door. "*Come on!* You've monopolized the bathroom for a whole hour. I've got to go get Julie in fifteen minutes."

"And Stony is going to be here any minute and I have to be ready," I countered, my hands trembling with excitement as I thought of the evening to come. Mom and Dad had left an hour ago to go out to dinner, seeming almost pleased that Jeff and I had other plans and they could enjoy a meal alone together.

"Okay, I'm done," I said, realizing there was nothing more I could do to get ready for my date. I opened the door and stepped out, giggling as Jeff shot into the bathroom and locked the door behind him.

I sat down at the kitchen table to wait for Stony, trying to control the nervousness that had suddenly gripped me. It had been a long day, and not a minute had gone by that I hadn't realized I was one minute closer to being on a date with Stony. Martha and I had stayed at the waterfall until almost noon, talking and laughing, trading stories about our families and friends. After eating lunch together, Martha headed home and I lay down and took a nap in anticipation of a late night tonight. When I woke up, it was time to start getting ready. I had hoped that my conversation with Martha would reveal more information about Stony. But she hadn't mentioned him again, and I was reluctant to press the topic. Now I was going to get to know him personally.

Boy, that thought really made me nervous. He was so attractive. I paused as a new thought struck me: Wouldn't it be wonderful if we could really grow to care about one another?

I thought about what Martha had said about

vacation romances, how they were so difficult to maintain once the vacation was over. *That may be true in some cases*, I thought to myself, *but surely there are some vacation romances that last a long time. After all, Stony lives in Durango, which is only about a five- or six-hour drive from where I live in Denver. Not so very far for weekend visits.*

I grinned at where my thoughts were leading. I hadn't even had my first date with him yet and already I had us commuting between Denver and Durango. I'd just have to wait and see how things developed. Tonight would either be the beginning of a wonderful romance or the end of my fantasies about Stony.

I heard someone knock at the door, and I took a deep breath. Stony was finally here!

Chapter Seven

"Hi, are you all ready to go?" Stony asked as I opened the door and greeted him.

I nodded and joined him on the sun deck.

"You look great," he said, his blue eyes sparkling.

"Thanks," I murmured with a small blush, suddenly feeling shy. It's funny—I'd been anxiously waiting all day for this moment to arrive, and now that it was here, I felt tongue-tied. Stony looked great, too. He was dressed in faded blue jeans that fit him like a second skin, showing off his long, muscular legs. His blue T-shirt was exactly the same color as his eyes. As he took my hand and pulled me closer to him, I could smell the clean, minty scent of soap and the subtle musk of the cologne he was wearing.

"I've never been to a campfire cookout before," I said as we began to walk along the path that led to the stables. *Oh great*, I thought, *that was a brilliant thing to say.*

Stony turned and looked at me incredulously. "What? No Girl Scout camps or summer camps that had campfires?"

I shook my head. "I was never a Girl Scout, and I never went to summer camp," I explained.

"Oh, you poor, deprived girl." Stony grinned at me, then dropped my hand and, much to my surprise, threw his arm around my shoulders. "I'll have to make sure that your very first campfire experience is a memorable one."

It already is, I thought breathlessly, enjoying the feel of Stony's arm around me.

"And I'll bet you've never been on a horse before, either," Stony continued, looking at me in amusement.

I shook my head. "There aren't many places where you can horseback ride in Denver. I've always wanted to learn to ride, but private lessons are so expensive."

"Well, you can come trail riding with me. I've got some places that I consider my very own, and I'd really like to share them with you," he said softly as he looked down at me.

I'd read in romance novels about women swooning, and I'd never been able to understand how a man could make a woman do that. But all of a sudden, I understood perfectly. Stony's words made my knees weaken, and my heart seemed to be missing beats. I felt light-headed and knew that I was probably as close to a swoon as I would ever be!

I was almost disappointed when we came to the stables. There were already a bunch of kids gathered there, and I knew my moments alone with Stony were over—for the time being.

I was surprised to see several groups of parents standing around, and I was grateful that mine had gone out to eat. How mortifying! I'd die if my parents showed up for the cookout and saw me there with Stony. "I didn't know the cookout was for adults, too," I said to Stony.

"Yeah, actually the cookouts are for everyone at the resort. The parents usually stay long enough to eat, then they leave, and the rest of the night belongs to us." He smiled down at me. "Come on, I'm sort of in charge of the cookouts, so I need to get things under control." He turned to the group of people. "Okay, folks. If you'll all follow me, I'll take you to our campfire site." He took my hand once again and led us all around the edge of the stable and into a small clearing, where two large coolers were sitting on the ground and firewood was neatly laid inside a circle of rocks.

"I've got to get the fire started." Stony smiled apologetically and dropped my hand. "Why don't you find us a place to sit at the edge of the fire site and I'll join you in a while."

I nodded and walked over to the place where the firewood was set up. I chose a spot next to the circle of rocks and sat down on the ground, my eyes following Stony as he walked away and got busy moving the coolers closer to the fire site. As I watched him, I suddenly thought about what Julie had said the day before when we had all been swimming. "Stony always gives special attention to all the new girls," she'd said. Was that what Stony was doing tonight? Merely paying special attention to the new girl? That was the last thing I wanted to believe.

"Hey, Kate!" Martha yelled to me as her family entered the clearing on the opposite side of the campfire from where I was sitting. Martha said something to her sister and her parents, then hurried over and plopped down next to me. "I'm so embarrassed!" she whispered in disgust. "This is the first year my parents decided to come to the cookout!"

"There are other parents here besides yours," I offered with a sympathetic smile.

"Huh, you can afford to say that—your parents aren't here!" Martha exclaimed.

I laughed at her look of disgust.

"Anyway," she continued more optimistically. "It's getting dark and maybe none of the other kids will know they're my parents, especially if I sit over here with you." She smiled at me brightly and I smiled back, but inside I felt a little stab of disappointment. I really liked Martha and all that, but my idea of a dream date with Stony didn't exactly include us sitting with Martha all night long.

At the thought of Stony, I scanned the crowd until I found him. He was lighting the fire, and I admired the way he seemed to know exactly which pieces of kindling to light to get the fire started. As the pile of twigs burst into flame, Stony's hair glistened, reflecting the reds and golds of the firelight. He looked across the fire, tilted his head in that cute way of his, and smiled at me. For a moment our gazes held. I caught my breath, knowing that no matter what happened in the future, I would remember this vacation and this night with Stony for the rest of my life.

Darkness had fallen, and the fire created an intimate circle of light. As the fire glowed on all our faces, I noticed that most of the kids I'd gone swimming with yesterday were here, although everyone seemed sort of subdued and quiet. I saw Julie and Jeff sitting next to each other on the opposite side of the fire, talking quietly with one another. *Susie would be really upset if she saw him now,* I thought. What in the world was Jeff doing flirting with Julie when he had a steady girlfriend back home?

"So, what'd you do this afternoon?" Martha asked.

"I took a nap," I admitted sheepishly.

"That was smart. Sometimes these campfires last until one or two in the morning." Martha rubbed her hands together with enthusiasm. "It just depends on how many of us have good ghost stories to tell."

I frowned at her words. I hate ghost stories almost as much as I hate horror movies. They scare me to death, and each time I swear I'm never going to see another one, but I'm addicted! I looked around the dark woods that surrounded us. A spooky story would be a lot spookier out here in the woods. It was easy to believe that the headless horseman or some other creepy specter might emerge from the woods at any moment. I shivered at this frightening thought.

"What's the matter?" Martha asked, seeing me shiver.

"Nothing. I was just thinking how scary it would be to tell ghost stories out here."

"Oh, it is!" Martha giggled. "I love being scared, don't you?"

I grinned at her. "Yeah, I guess I do," I agreed.

"Okay guys, soup's on! Help yourselves," Stony yelled to everyone, going over to the coolers and opening them up. As people began to crowd around the coolers, grabbing sodas, long sticks, and hot dogs, Stony came back and sat down next to me.

"Sorry about that, but I had to get everything ready. It's part of my job." He smiled at me.

"No problem," I smiled back, thinking I'd forgive Stony for just about anything to see his gorgeous smile.

"For the rest of the night, I'm all yours. There's nothing I have to do except enjoy being with you." His smile was soft and sexy looking, and once again my heart began to skip beats. I found myself wondering if a teenage girl could die from this condition.

"Uh . . . I think I'll go get a hot dog," Martha said, sounding slightly uncomfortable as she looked first at me, then at Stony.

"Are you hungry?" Stony asked me as Martha got up and went over to the coolers.

"Not really, not yet," I answered. "But you go ahead and eat if you want to."

"Nah, I'll wait for you. There's quite a crowd anyway," he said, watching as about ten people crowded around the open fire, hot dogs stuck on sticks.

The food seemed to liven up the crowd, and the clearing filled with the gentle hum of people talking and laughing. The air smelled good, a combination of pine trees and cooking hot dogs.

Stony said something, but I couldn't hear him, because the rest of the group at the fire was laughing. Sam's hot dog had fallen off his stick, sizzling loudly as it hit the fire.

"Pardon me?" I said, leaning closer to him.

"I said your hair really looks pretty in the

firelight." He reached up and fingered a strand of my hair gently.

"Thanks," I said shyly. "Your hair looks nice, too. It's so blond!"

Stony reached up and touched his white-blond hair with a rueful grin. "I used to hate my hair," he confessed with a little laugh.

"Why?" I asked incredulously. "I know a dozen girls who would gladly chop off their arms to have hair like yours."

"When I was really young, not only was my hair this blond, but it was also really curly. My mom had me wear it long because she loved my blond curls. How I hated them! All the kids at school teased me about my girly curls, and I was always having fights with them. Mom didn't realize how bad it was until the third grade. I found her scissors and really did a number on my hair." He laughed at the memory. "I think I was the first guy to have a punk hairstyle. By the time I was finished, it was about a thousand different lengths, all sticking straight out on end!"

I giggled at the mental image I had of him as a young punker. "Just think—you probably started the whole punk-rock movement," I teased.

"Yeah, but now I've decided to keep it short enough so it doesn't curl at all," he finished with a grin.

"Sometimes I think it would be much easier if everyone in the world was bald," I said thoughtfully, thinking of all the times I'd cursed my hair because it wouldn't do what I'd wanted it to.

"I'll tell you what we can do," Stony's grin widened, causing the cleft in his chin to deepen. "We can go back to my room and shave our heads and see if the fad catches on."

"Okay," I agreed, then added with a giggle. "But we'll shave your head first—*then* I'll make up my mind if I want mine done."

"I knew you were sneaky when I first saw you." Stony laughed and took my hand in his, then looked at me intently. "You know, you have gorgeous eyes. They're the prettiest green, like a cat's eyes." He squeezed my hand. "That's what I'll call you: Cat!"

I smiled at him. Cat . . . I liked it. Nobody had ever made up a special nickname for me before.

"Are you ready to get something to eat now? There's nothing better than hot dogs cooked over an open fire."

"Okay," I agreed, allowing him to pull me to my feet. I waved to Martha, who was talking with her sister. Stony led me over to the cooler, where Jeff and Julie were putting hot dogs on sticks. "Hi, guys," I greeted them, taking one of the sticks and grabbing a hot dog from the cooler.

"Hi, Kate." Julie smiled at me, but she didn't

bother to greet Stony. Then she turned her attention back to her hot dog.

"Have you done any fishing yet?" Stony asked Jeff as he fixed his hot dog.

"A little bit this afternoon, but I didn't have much luck," Jeff answered.

"Maybe one day this week I can take you out on the boat and show you some of the good spots," Stony offered.

"That would be great!" Jeff said enthusiastically. "Just let me know when you have the time and I'll be ready."

"That was really nice of you," I said to Stony, as Jeff and Julie moved away from the coolers and over to the fire.

Stony smiled at me. "Part of my job is to keep the guests happy," he explained, then added, "Besides, I figure it can't hurt to get on the good side of your brother. That way if I make you mad, maybe he won't beat me up!"

I laughed at this, unable to imagine Jeff beating up anyone, especially for my benefit. "You don't have to worry about Jeff. He's not the protective type. If you make me mad, *I'll* be the one who will personally beat you up!" I warned him, giggling as he looked at me with a silly, petrified expression.

"Do me a favor?" Stony looked at me pleadingly.

"What?" I asked.

"Let me know if I start to make you mad—then I'll know when to duck!"

"It's a deal." I grinned, liking Stony more every minute I spent with him.

"Now, let's get these hot dogs cooked. I'm starving!" With this, Stony put his arm around my shoulders again and led me to the fire.

"They taste twice as good as they smell," he promised.

"Hey Stony, are you gonna sing for us later?" Johnny called over from where he was sitting with Martha, Mary, and their parents.

"Sure," Stony agreed. "But wait until after I eat. I always sing flat on an empty stomach."

"You build fires, cook hot dogs, *and* sing as well?" I smiled up at Stony. "You're a guy of many talents."

"Now I'll demonstrate my talent for eating." He grinned, pulling his hot dog out of the fire.

I chuckled and followed him over to the coolers, where we fixed our hot dogs with relishes and buns.

As Stony had predicted, after we'd all eaten our fill, the parents drifted back to their cabins. I had a sense that now the evening would *really* begin.

We all gathered around the fire, sitting as close as we could without getting scorched. It was a strange feeling, the cool night air on my back and the front of my body all toasty and warm. My whole body grew warm as Stony put an arm around my shoulders and pulled me close. For a while we sat silently, nobody really saying much of anything, everyone just enjoying the beauty of the fire and the still night that surrounded us.

I felt like I had somehow drifted into one of my very best dreams. True, my daydreams about this vacation had been set on a beach. But, sitting here with Stony, staring into the flames of the fire, I couldn't remember what the attraction of a surfer guy had been.

"What are you thinking about?" Stony asked me, his breath soft and warm against my forehead.

"Oh, I was just thinking about how glad I am that we came to Lake Vallecito," I said, looking up into his blue eyes and thinking about how easy it was to be mesmerized by them.

"I'm really glad you came, too." Stony's gaze held mine, and my heart thudded wildly with the thought that he was going to kiss me. His lips were mere inches away from mine, and he was looking intently at me. But the moment was broken abruptly as a loud scream filled the clearing and a short, dirty-faced kid jumped out of a nearby tree.

"Oh Randy, what are you doing here?" Sam groaned along with several other kids. "You're supposed to be up at the cabin with Mom and Dad."

"Who's that?" I whispered to Stony.

"That's Sam's little brother. He's a cross between Dennis the Menace and Rambo," Stony explained.

"Randy, do Mom and Dad know you're out here?" Sam demanded.

"Nah, I crawled out the window," Randy replied, grinning at the group and displaying a missing front tooth. His gaze suddenly fell on me. "You're new here," he announced, and I nodded and smiled at him. "Are you Stony's girlfriend?"

I blushed and looked down at my hands.

"Are you and Stony going to kiss later?" he continued, making everyone laugh but me.

If my blush gets any redder, everybody will think I'm a tomato, I thought desperately.

"All right, that's enough!" Sam stood up and grabbed his little brother and threw him over his shoulder. "I'll be right back," he said to the group.

"That kid is something else!" Martha said, grinning over at me sympathetically.

"Remember last year, when he thought the stables were too small for the horses, so he let all of them out?" Johnny laughed.

"I sure do remember," Stony replied with a groan. "It took me over three hours to round up the horses and get them back in their stalls!"

"Hey, Stony, you promised us a song!" Johnny said.

"I just happen to have my guitar right here," Stony said, jumping up and grabbing a guitar that was leaning against a nearby tree. "Why don't we start out with a warm-up song we can all sing together," he suggested, sitting back down next to me. He started strumming the melody to "Michael Row the Boat Ashore," and we all began to sing.

By the time we finished the song, Sam had returned without his little brother. He passed around a bag of marshmallows to toast, and we all launched into a rousing rendition of a popular rock song.

As the night went along and we all sang folk songs and ballads, I felt somehow connected to the others. It was almost as if in sharing this experience, we were touching each others' lives in a very special way. I knew I was being sentimental, but it's the way I felt as we all sang and smiled with one another.

The time grew later, and our songs grew slower. We had just finished singing "Down in the Valley" when Christy made a request.

"You sing for us, Stony," she said.

"Yeah, it's time for a solo!" Johnny echoed.

Stony nodded and began to sing a slow country song I'd never heard before. His voice was beautiful, rich and deep, and I was awed by his obvious talent. When he finished, we were all silent for a moment, allowing his last note to linger in the air, pure and sweet. I'd always thought country music wasn't my thing, but never had country music seemed as beautiful as it did at that moment.

"Sing another one," I said to Stony.

He nodded and sang another country song, one about a lost love and broken hearts. As he sang, I followed his changing expressions, enjoying the way he seemed to feel the emotions that were in the words of the song. I pulled my knees up to my chin, and rested my head on my arms, watching him play, proud to be his date. When the song was finished, once again there was a hushed silence from the crowd.

"Well, gang, we'd better wrap this up," Stony finally said, breaking the silence. "It's after one o'clock and I've got an early day tomorrow."

Everyone nodded and began to rise, as if Stony's words were the official ending of the night. Stony and I waited until everyone had left the clearing, then I watched as he put out the fire and packed everything back into the coolers.

"Did you have a good time tonight?" he asked as we started back on the dark path that led to my cabin.

"I had a *great* time tonight," I answered, hanging onto his arm in the darkness.

"I'm glad," he said. "I wanted you to have a good time, especially since it was your very first cookout."

"Well, I had a great time, and you are a

really good singer!" I looked up at him with admiration.

"Thanks. I really like to sing," he said, and I was impressed that he had no false modesty. I can't stand it when somebody doesn't know how to graciously accept a compliment.

"Have you ever thought about being a professional singer?" I asked, hating the sight of our cabin up ahead. Once we got there, my night with Stony would be over.

"No. I like to sing for pleasure, not when somebody pays me to sing," he explained.

"So, what do you want to be when you grow up?" I asked, smiling at how juvenile the question sounded.

Stony's laughter made a pleasant rumbling sound. "Ever since I was little, there's only been one thing I wanted to be—a cowboy. Now that I'm older and wiser, I still want to be a cowboy." He tilted his head in that endearing way and grinned down at me. "Actually, I'd like to be a rancher and own some acreage up here in the mountains."

"That sounds nice . . . I don't know what I want to be yet," I said, smiling to myself as Stony draped his arm around me, pulling me close to him. "I used to want to be a ballerina, but I've got two left feet. Then I thought I'd like to be a doctor—until last year when we dissected a frog in biology!"

Stony laughed. "I think we both have plenty of time to make decisions about what we want to be." We came to the steps that led to our sun deck. "Can you sit out here for a minute?" he asked.

"Sure," I answered, secretly thrilled. We sat down side by side on the second step. He hugged me close to him.

"It sure is a pretty night," I observed, able to see the moon reflecting on the nearby lake.

"I've never known a night that isn't beautiful out here," Stony replied.

"You love it here, don't you," I said softly.

Stony nodded. "I think this place has got to be as close to heaven as you can get." He gave a little self-conscious laugh. "I guess that sounds sort of stupid."

"No, it doesn't," I protested. "When Mom and Dad first told me we were coming here, I was really disappointed. I'd wanted to go to the beach. But I had no idea it was so pretty here." *And I had no idea I'd meet somebody like you,* I added silently.

"I like the beach, too. But Lake Vallecito will always be my first choice," Stony replied. "Especially right now." He smiled at me, then laughed. "Even in the moonlight I can see that you're blushing."

"I hate it when I blush," I said, covering my cheeks with my hands.

"I think it's cute," Stony answered me. "So tell me, Cat, what do you like to do when you're not blushing?"

I shrugged. "I spend a lot of time with my

best friend, Marcia. We go to movies, and do a lot of bike riding."

"If you like to bike ride, you'll love horseback riding," Stony exclaimed. "I'd rather ride a horse than ride in a car."

"I'll bet you're a really good horseback rider," I said, remembering how he'd looked like he belonged on his big, black horse the first day I'd seen him.

Stony smiled. "I'm not sure how good I am—I just love horses. They're so much less complicated than cars. You feed them, water them, and they'll take you wherever you want to go. And if you're affectionate to your horse, he's affectionate back. I've yet to see an affectionate car!"

I laughed in agreement. "I guess I'd better get inside," I said reluctantly, "though I hate to put a stop to such a fun evening."

"Yeah, it is getting kind of late." Stony and I stood up and walked over to the cabin door.

"Well, I guess this is goodbye," I said softly, wondering if I'd seen the last of Stony.

"Not goodbye, just goodnight," Stony corrected me. He pulled me closer to him, and his lips slowly met mine in a kiss so warm and sweet that it left me breathless.

"I've got to work all day tomorrow, but I'll try to come by and see you," he said as his lips left mine. "Till tomorrow," he whispered in my ear before releasing me. He jumped down off the sun deck and disappeared into the night.

I stood on the deck for a few minutes, replaying the night in minute detail. Stony was everything and more than I could ever have wanted in a guy. He was handsome, nice, talented, and so smooth. I reached up and touched my lips where he had kissed me. It had definitely been an A-1 great kiss!

"Till tomorrow." I repeated his parting words with a smile. My heart began beating again in that funny way, and I sighed as I turned and entered our cabin.

Chapter Eight

"Did you kids have a good time last night at your cookout?" Mom asked at breakfast the next morning.

"Yeah, but I can't believe you made us get up so early to have breakfast with you," I grumbled.

"For once, I agree with my sister," Jeff muttered from across the small dinette table. "I think it stinks that you woke us up at seven this morning!"

"What a couple of grouches!" Dad exclaimed. Jeff and I looked at each other sheepishly.

"Actually, we got you up early to have breakfast with us for a reason," Mom explained, setting a large platter of freshly cooked pancakes and sausages in the middle of the table. "We'd like to talk to you about a little side trip we'd like to take."

"A side trip? Away from Hidden Ranch? I don't have to go, do I? I'll die if I have to go with you!" I looked first at Mom, then at Dad, panic-stricken at the thought of spending any time away from Hidden Ranch. We only had eight more days left of vacation and I wanted to take advantage of every second I had left with Stony.

"My goodness, Kate, don't get hysterical." Mom laughed. "That's exactly what we wanted to discuss. Your dad and I thought we'd drive into Durango and spend a couple of days there. You two can either come with us or you can stay here if you wish."

"I'll stay here!" I said firmly, no doubt at all in my mind about what I wanted to do.

"And I guess I'd better stay here and baby-sit Kate," Jeff replied, half-teasingly.

"Ha! You mean you'll stay here and baby-sit Julie," I retorted, then added, "Wait until Susie hears about your hot new romance!"

Jeff shot me a look of disgust. "I'm not having a *hot new romance,*" he protested. "Julie and I are just friends."

"Yeah, sure," I smirked. "You looked plenty friendly last night, snuggling together by the campfire!"

"You always exaggerate everything!" Jeff said accusingly. "Why don't you just mind your own business."

"I want you to keep an eye on each other while we're gone," Mom interrupted us. Jeff and I stopped arguing—for the moment—and nodded.

"Yoo-hoo, anyone here?" There was a knock on the door, and I recognized Martha's voice.

"That's Martha," I said, jumping up from the table and going to the door.

"Hi," Martha greeted me with a bright smile. "I went to your window, but when you didn't answer I thought you might be up already, surprisingly enough."

"We're eating breakfast. Come on in." I opened the cabin door and let her in. "Mom, Dad, this is Martha."

"We met your sister and your parents out on the lake yesterday." Mom smiled at Martha. "Why don't you join us for some pancakes?"

Martha looked hesitantly at the large stack. "Well, maybe just one," she said, pulling a chair up to the table and sitting down.

Martha ate four pancakes, managing to talk nonstop in between each bite. Jeff and Dad went back to their pancakes, allowing Martha, Mom, and me to monopolize the conversation.

"You really should talk to Stony if you're going to visit Durango," Martha said after Mom told her about the side trip. "He lives in Durango and can tell you all about what to see and where to go."

"That's a wonderful idea," Mom said enthusiastically. "I'd really like a chance to talk to him before we leave."

"He's supposed to stop by sometime today,"

I said, feeling the heat rise to my face. "But he didn't say exactly when."

"I hope he comes by before noon. If not, maybe your father and I can find him before we leave this afternoon," Mom said.

Dad nodded in agreement, then stood up from the table. "I think I'll get in a little fishing before we leave this afternoon."

"Want some company?" Jeff asked.

"Sure," Dad said, obviously pleased. Together, the two of them left the cabin.

"I'll take care of the dishes," Mom said as I started clearing the table.

"Thanks." I gave my mom a hug, then turned to Martha. "Let's go to my room. I want to change clothes and get cleaned up." Martha followed me into my small bedroom and sat down on the edge of the bed, watching as I dug through my suitcase to find something decent to wear. I wanted to look good when Stony stopped by.

"So, did you have fun last night?" Martha asked slyly.

"I had a great time." I looked at her and grinned, knowing I must look really dopey.

"I thought you and Stony looked pretty happy together. When I got up to get a hot dog, I moved to the other side of the fire to give you guys some time alone," she said, the sly grin still covering her face.

"I noticed, and you have my undying gratitude." I laughed, pulling a pair of pale blue shorts and a cropped, peach-colored T-shirt from the suitcase.

"So, did he kiss you?" she asked.

"Martha!" I exclaimed in mock outrage, unsure if I wanted a girl I'd only met two days earlier to know the intimate details of my romantic life.

"Oh, come on, Kate. You have to tell me everything." Martha smiled with a touch of wistfulness. "When you've never had a real date, the only romance you get is listening to friends talk about their love lives."

I thought about what she said, and relented. "Yeah, he kissed me." I grinned as she squealed and clapped her hands together.

"Was it amazing?" Martha asked eagerly.

I laughed happily. "Yeah, it was pretty wonderful." I sat down next to her on the bed and gazed at her seriously. "Oh, Martha, I think I'm really beginning to like Stony a lot, and it's kind of scary."

"Scary? Why?" Martha looked at me curiously.

"It's a vacation romance," I answered, sighing impatiently as she looked at me blankly. "Well, you said it yourself the other day—summer romances are too hard to maintain once the vacation is over."

"Jeez, Kate, don't listen to me," Martha protested. "What do I know about romance, summer vacation or any other kind!"

"But what you said makes a lot of sense," I

retorted unhappily. I looked down at the T-shirt in my lap, idly picking at the raised lettering that read Colorado University. "I don't want to fall wildly in love with Stony, only to have it all end in eight days when we go back home. That would hurt too much."

Martha was silent for a moment. "Look, Kate," she finally said. "You live in Denver, right? And Stony lives in Durango," she continued. "That's about a five- or six-hour drive to Denver, right?"

"Right," I agreed.

"Well, that's not so far away! You can see each other pretty often," Martha exclaimed brightly. "I say go for it, Kate! Stony's such a nice guy—and cute too!"

I grinned, knowing that's exactly what I'd intended to do all along. Sure, there was the definite possibility that this thing with Stony would fizzle out after I returned home, but there was also the possibility that Stony and I could develop a special, lasting relationship. At the moment, I was feeling pretty optimistic. After all, I'd had a wonderful time last night, and I think Stony did, too.

"Actually, I stopped by to tell you that a bunch of us are going to rent paddleboats this afternoon. Do you want to come?" Martha asked.

I hesitated. It sounded like fun, but I wasn't going to budge from this cabin until Stony came by. I didn't want to miss him. "I don't know . . . maybe . . . What time is everyone going?"

"We're meeting at the stables around noon," Martha answered.

"If I decide to go, I'll meet you there," I said, standing up and gathering my clothes.

"I'll get out of here so you can get changed." Martha jumped off my bed. "I've got to get back to our cabin. I didn't even tell Mom and Dad where I was going." With a wave, she left.

The next few hours felt like weeks. I paced the cabin, unable to occupy myself with anything for more than five minutes at a time. It was almost noon when Stony finally stopped by. I was in my room writing a letter to Marcia when Mom knocked on my door. "Kate, Stony's here."

"I'll be out in just a minute," I answered. My first impulse was to fly out of the bedroom, but I didn't want to appear too anxious. So instead I slowly counted to ten as I stood next to my door, then calmly opened it and walked out into the kitchen.

"Hi." I smiled shyly at Stony, who was sitting at the table across from my mom. Every time I saw him I was struck again by how handsome he was.

"Stony was just filling me in on Durango," Mom said. "Did you know that Durango has an operating steam engine that pulls a train through the San Juan Mountains to Silverton?

Stony's been telling me that most of the cars are furnished with authentic 1880 pieces." Mom's eyes sparkled with excitement.

"Sounds right up your alley." I smiled at Mom and joined them at the table. "Mom's really into antiques," I explained to Stony. "She owns an antique store."

"You should get in touch with my mother," Stony replied. "She's really into antiques and knows the places to get the best deals. If you have a piece of paper, I'll be glad to write down her name and phone number."

"Are you sure your mother wouldn't mind talking to me?" Mom looked at him hopefully.

"Not at all. Mom likes to talk to other antique fanatics." Stony and I laughed as Mom quickly grabbed her purse and pulled out a sheet of paper.

"Well, I'd better get back to work," Stony said after he'd given Mom the information.

"Oh, okay." I swallowed my disappointment. *He just got here!* I thought. *Why does he have to leave so soon?*

As we stepped out onto the sun deck, Stony turned and faced me with a soft smile. "Actually, I stopped by for a specific reason."

"You had a sudden urge to tell my mom about Durango?" I teased, enjoying the sound of his laughter.

"No, I ran into Jeff and your dad out fishing a little while ago, and Jeff told me that he and Julie are going to the Double O Saloon for some dancing. I was wondering if you'd like to go with me tonight?"

"Sure, it'll be sort of like a double date," I answered with a smile, trying to imagine what it would be like to dance with Stony, to be held in his arms for song after song. . . .

"Great!" He tilted his head to one side and grinned at me happily. "Jeff said he and Julie were leaving here about seven, so I'll come by for you then, okay?"

"Okay," I answered. Double okay! Triple okay! Another date with Stony! *I hope I get a chance to write Marcia before I die of happiness*, I thought to myself.

"Well, I gotta go." He grinned crookedly, then jumped off the sun deck and disappeared into the woods.

I watched him go, feeling a funny sensation in the pit of my stomach. Even though I'd never felt that way before, I knew immediately what it meant—I was well on my way to falling in love with Steve Mahoney!

Chapter Nine

As I got ready for a night of dancing at the Double O, I tried to keep my excitement in check. I know I have a tendency to exaggerate situations, like Jeff said, but I couldn't help but think that Stony must really like me. After all, nobody had twisted his arm to ask me out again. I smiled at my reflection in the mirror, remembering the way Stony had looked at me and the way he had kissed me—and I just knew he cared about me. But how much? True, we'd only known each other for a couple of days, but I felt differently about him than anyone I'd ever known before.

"Kate, I'm going to get Julie," Jeff called from the kitchen, interrupting my thoughts. "We'll be back here in a few minutes."

"Okay," I yelled back. I turned away from the mirror, finally satisfied with my appearance. I was wearing a pink sundress, not as cute as Marcia's blue one, but the best outfit I'd brought along.

"Hello? Cat?"

I ran to the cabin door as soon as I heard Stony's voice.

"Hi." I smiled happily, and opened the door to let him in. "Jeff went to get Julie. They'll be here in a minute."

"Then we'd better take advantage of this moment alone," Stony said, and placing his hands on either side of my face, he kissed me soundly. "Hmm, you taste as sweet as candy," he said, making me giggle as he smacked his lips together.

"You don't taste so bad yourself," I responded. I couldn't help it; being around Stony turned me into such a flirt!

Stony grabbed my arm and twirled me around. "You look as pretty as a flower in full bloom!"

"Ah, silver-tongued Stony strikes again. Some things never change," Julie said dryly, entering the cabin in front of Jeff.

There was a moment of awkward silence as Stony and Julie eyed each other warily.

"Are we all ready to go?" I asked brightly, ready to do just about anything to dispel the tension in the air. Something was definitely wrong between the two of them, but I didn't want anything to ruin my night with Stony. I turned and gave Julie a pleading look. *Please don't ruin things tonight,* I tried to communicate to her.

Julie flushed slightly beneath my gaze, and grabbed Jeff's hand. "Let's go," she exclaimed, and I heaved a sigh of relief.

The walk to the Double O Saloon took about fifteen minutes, and I was grateful that Jeff and Julie walked briskly, leaving Stony and me behind. We walked slowly and silently, but it was a nice kind of quiet.

"I'm glad that you're not the kind of girl who has to fill every second with conversation," Stony said, obviously aware of the silence between us too.

"Sometimes it's kind of nice to be quiet and just enjoy being together," I said seriously.

Stony stopped walking and turned to look at me. His gaze was thoughtful and serious. Then he smiled gently at me. "You know, you're a very nice kind of girl." He took my hand and we continued walking.

"I'm looking forward to dancing with you," he said after another moment of silence. "Dancing gives me a legitimate excuse to put my arms around you."

I looked up at him, smiling softly. "What makes you think you need a legitimate excuse?" I asked him teasingly. He grinned back at me—that sexy smile that made my knees wobble and my face flush—as we entered the lighted parking area of the Double O.

The Double O was like no other place I'd

ever been before. As Stony opened the door for me, the first thing that struck me was the sounds of a live band performing a rousing country song. We stepped inside, and I felt my excitement grow as I looked around and felt the energy and enthusiasm of the crowd inside.

Jeff and Julie motioned to us from a booth where they were seated, and we made our way toward them through the throng of people.

"Whew, what a crowd!" Stony exclaimed as I slid into the red leather booth and he slid in next to me.

"This is a great place!" I replied, looking at the large dance floor crowded with people dancing to the beat of the band.

"The first time I came here, I thought it was sort of square—you know, the country music and all that," Julie said. "But since then I've actually gotten into country music back home."

"It's not too bad," Jeff agreed, smiling at the waitress who appeared at our table. Jeff, Julie, and Stony all ordered full meals, but I was too excited to eat, so I only ordered a soda.

"Wow, what a cheap date." Stony grinned at me as the waitress left our table.

I shrugged. "I'm just not hungry."

"It's a good thing she isn't," Jeff said. "Otherwise we might all have had to wash dishes to pay for everything Kate can eat!" Everyone laughed except me, and I glared at Jeff. I couldn't believe he'd made me sound like a total pig in front of Stony. There is definitely a down side to double-dating with your brother!

"You wanna dance?" Stony asked me.

I looked out at the dance floor, where everyone seemed to know exactly what they were doing. I'd never tried dancing to country music before. In fact, I hadn't done much dancing at all. "I don't know," I answered hesitantly. "I'll bet you're a real good dancer, aren't you?" I asked Stony.

"Stony is an expert at all the social skills—dancing and giving compliments are his specialties. He's had a lot of practice," Julie said with an unpleasant little smile.

"Knock it off, Julie," Stony said in a low voice. Then he looked at me. "Come on, let's dance." He touched my arm, as if anxious to get away from Julie.

As soon as we got out onto the dance floor, the music ended. "We'll wait for the next one," Stony said. Immediately, the band began a slow number, and his arms drew me close as we began to sway to the music.

We fit together perfectly. I know this sounds sort of silly, but it's true. Stony's mouth was near my forehead, making his shoulders just the right height for me to put my arms around his neck. I was immediately aware of how good it felt to be close to him. I could smell the scent of his cologne, a lingering smell of shaving cream, and the clean smell of freshly shampooed hair. And I could feel the muscles in his shoulders move beneath my hands as he shifted his weight from side to side.

I tried to put everything else out of my mind and enjoy the moment, but I just couldn't relax completely. My mind filled with questions about him and Julie. What exactly was going on between them? Was it simply a case of Julie not liking Stony? That couldn't be it—she seemed to go out of her way to say hateful things to him. I wished I could ask Stony what the deal was between him and Julie, but I didn't feel like breaking the mood.

"You're a good dancer," Stony said, smiling down at me. His lips touched my forehead gently, and I closed my eyes and lay my head on his shoulder, happier than I'd ever been in my entire life.

I wished the song would last forever, but it came to an end all too soon and the band began to play a fast tune. I shook my head and started to head for our table as Stony urged me to join him for another dance. "Come on," he said, tugging me back out onto the dance floor. "I'll teach you the two-step," he promised, laughing as I looked at him dubiously.

"I told you last night that I have two left feet—that's why I could never be a ballerina!" I protested.

"Oh, come on, you're exaggerating, everyone can two-step!" Stony laughed and took me in his arms.

He's right! I can two-step, I thought in amazement as he began to move in fluid steps that were easy to follow. I caught on quickly, enjoying the upbeat rhythm of the dance. Dancing was fun!

"Not too shabby," he said, grinning at me when the dance was over. "You only stepped on my toes ten times." He laughed as I elbowed him lightly in the ribs.

"I did not," I protested, allowing him to lead me back to our table, where Julie and Jeff were eating their dinners.

As we all sat there at the table, I once again found myself wondering what was going on between Julie and Stony. Julie avoided looking at Stony, and kept her conversation directed at Jeff and me. And Stony didn't talk to her, either. It was like Julie and Stony just happened to be sitting in the same booth.

"I think I'll go get another soda," Stony said, interrupting my thoughts. "You want another one?"

I shook my head.

"I'll go with you. I could use another one myself," Jeff said, and together the two guys left for the bar.

"Your brother is really nice," Julie commented to me once they were gone.

"He's all right," I answered. Then, taking a

deep breath, I plunged ahead, determined to ask her the burning question. "Julie . . . is there something going on between you and Stony?"

"Of course not," she answered quickly, a deep flush coloring her face. "What could possibly be going on between Stony and me? That's ridiculous!" Her eyes didn't meet mine.

She's lying, a small voice said inside my head. *She's lying and I don't know why.* Had they been going out and broke up before we came? Was Stony just using me to make Julie jealous? My mind whirled with all kinds of questions. The only thing that seemed crystal clear to me was that, for some reason, Julie was lying.

"Here we are."

I looked up as Stony and Jeff slid back into the booth. Stony took a long sip of his soda, then grinned at me. "Are you ready to tear up the dance floor some more?"

"Okay," I agreed. Dismissing Julie's odd behavior from my mind, I followed Stony out onto the dance floor.

All too soon, just as I began to get the hang of the new steps, Jeff found us on the dance floor and told us he was taking Julie home. Stony and I finished our dance, then started the walk back to the resort.

"My vacation is almost half over," I said as we walked slowly down the road. "I've only got six more days here and then I'll be back in Denver." I sighed, depressed at this thought.

"Are you going to think about me when you get back home?" Stony asked softly.

"It depends," I answered teasingly. "Are you going to think about me?" I held my breath, waiting for his answer. Of course, even if he had said I would never cross his mind once I was gone, I knew he would never be very far from my thoughts—no matter where I was.

He stopped walking and pulled me in front of him. The moon was brilliant overhead and we could see each other perfectly. "Kate Weatherby, I'm going to think about you a lot." He brushed a strand of hair off my forehead, and looked at me intently, as if he were trying to memorize every feature. I didn't have to memorize the way he looked—I couldn't forget him if I tried. "When I first saw you sleeping on the beach, I sat down next to you and stared at you for a long time before I decided to wake you up."

I blushed at the thought of him watching me while I slept. "Was I snoring or something?" I asked with a self-conscious smile.

"No, you weren't snoring." Stony laughed softly. "That first time I saw you, I knew deep inside you were going to be special to me." He looked at me, his eyes searching my face. "Did you feel anything like that?" he asked, sounding almost worried about what my answer was going to be.

"Yes," I answered breathlessly. "Now what do we do?" I asked as we continued to look at each other.

"I think this is the part where I'm supposed to kiss you," Stony teased.

"Well, don't you think you'd better do what you're supposed to do?" I asked, blushing as I realized I was practically asking him to kiss me. I sighed with happiness as he did. His soft, lingering kiss stole my breath away.

"Kate, I want to spend every spare minute I have with you for the next six days," Stony said as his lips left mine.

"I'd like that, Stony," I responded.

"How about if we start tomorrow morning," he said. "Tomorrow is my day off, and I'd like to spend the day with you."

"Okay." I smiled, wondering if he could hear the loud beating of my heart.

"I'll come by for you in the morning. I've got some very special places I'd like to share with you."

I nodded as we came to our cabin and walked up the stairs to the sun deck. "I'll be ready," I promised.

I paused at the door of our cabin, turning back to him one more time. "Well, goodnight," I said softly.

"Goodnight, Cat." He leaned down and gently kissed me goodnight. I watched him leave until he had disappeared, swallowed up by the darkness of the night. I felt a little flushed, but I also felt cold and shivery. I'd never been in love before, and I wondered if that was what I was feeling right now.

I sighed and went into the cabin, thinking of everything that I would add to the letter I'd been writing to Marcia earlier in the day. *And to think I wanted to go to the beach!* I laughed, thrilled that we had come to boring Lake Vallecito after all!

Chapter Ten

"Kate! Hey, Kate."

I opened my eyes and stared at the darkness of the room, knowing something had woken me up, but unsure exactly what it was.

"Hey, Kate, are you in there?"

That's what woke me—a voice coming from outside my window! I scrambled out of bed and stumbled through the darkness of the room.

"Stony?" I said as soon as I saw the moonlight shining on his pale hair. "What are you doing here! It's the middle of the night!"

Stony laughed. "It's not the middle of the night. It's almost morning."

I yawned. "Boy, when you said 'morning' you weren't kidding."

"I thought you'd like to see the sunrise with me," he said, smiling sheepishly.

My breath caught in my throat. How romantic, to watch the sun come up with Stony! "That sounds great!" I said excitedly, all traces of sleepiness completely gone.

"Well then, come on!" Stony laughed again. "The sun waits for nobody."

I dressed in the darkness, pulling on a pair of faded jeans and a cotton shirt, then ran into the bathroom to wash my face, clean my teeth, and brush my hair.

I started to sneak past Jeff, not wanting to wake him up, then decided I'd better let him know what my plans were. Whenever Mom and Dad leave Jeff in charge, he takes his newfound responsibility very seriously. If he woke up and found me gone without a note or anything, he'd probably call the FBI and have them out hunting for me! I quickly scribbled Jeff a note and stuck it on the refrigerator door, knowing that was always the first place he looked when he woke up.

I grabbed my denim jacket and stepped outside into the chill, predawn darkness.

"Good morning." Stony met me on the sun deck, his teeth gleaming in the moonlight as he grinned at me. "Come on, I've got the horses all saddled up and ready."

"Horses? Stony, you do remember that I've never ridden before," I reminded him as we began to walk toward the stables.

"I remember." He smiled. "Don't worry, I

picked out the gentlest mare we have. Her name is Sweetheart and she's perfect for you."

"I just think it would be nice if one of us, the horse or myself, knew what we were doing!" I said, shivering with excitement.

"Cold?" Stony put an arm around my shoulder. When he pulled me close to him, there was no way I was going to admit that it was excitement and not the morning chill that had made me shiver.

Outside the stables, two horses were stomping the ground impatiently. "This one is Sweetheart," he said, patting the smaller of the two horses.

I eyed the chestnut horse dubiously. "Hi, Sweetheart," I said.

"You already said hi to me," Stony teased.

I giggled. "I was talking to my horse."

"We'd better get started or we're going to miss the sunrise," Stony said. "Can you mount your horse, or do you want me to help you?"

"I can do it," I said recklessly. After all, I've seen hundreds of Western movies and getting on a horse always looks so easy.

Unfortunately, it wasn't. I put my foot in the stirrup and tried to pull myself up and over the horse's back. Nobody in those Westerns ever said anything about the pull of gravity. At that moment, gravity seemed to have a firm hold on my bottom, making it impossible to swing up over the horse.

I hung in midair for what seemed like an eternity, then blushed furiously as Stony gave my rear a shove that sent me over the top of the horse and into the saddle. "Thanks," I murmured, my blush deepening as I saw his look of amusement.

"*Any* time," he answered, then walked over to his horse and swung himself into the saddle with an ease that would have put John Wayne to shame. "Sweetheart will follow Manny," Stony explained, patting his own horse's neck, the same big black horse he'd been riding the very first time I saw him. He took off at a slow walk and Sweetheart immediately followed behind him.

We followed a path that I hadn't yet explored. As we rode we didn't speak, except for Stony warning me about low-hanging branches or telling me how to hold the reins. There was something mysterious and romantic about riding horses through the woods in the darkness of the early morning. The birds were just beginning to awaken and were chirping their early-morning songs.

I don't know how long we had ridden when suddenly we came to the end of the woods and I realized we were on a large bluff overlooking a valley. Stony got off his horse and came over to help me off mine. I must admit I was grateful for his help—my legs were pretty wobbly! He then took a rolled-up blanket from the back of his saddle and spread it out on the ground.

"I see you came prepared," I observed.

"I used to be a Boy Scout," he quipped. He smiled and sat down on the blanket, then patted the spot next to him. "You are about to see one of the most spectacular sights," he said as I sat down next to him on the blanket.

"It's beautiful up here," I said as the sky lightened a bit more and I was able to see the green valley below.

"Yeah, this is one of my favorite places." Stony looked at me intently, reminding me that I didn't have any makeup on. "I only bring special people up here with me," he said softly, putting his arm around me.

"And I'm a special person?" I asked, slightly breathless.

"I think you are," he answered. His lips moved softly over mine. Stony's kisses were different from anyone else's in the world. Some guys kiss so rough, you feel like your teeth are being shoved through your lips. Others barely touch your lips, like they don't know exactly what they're doing—and they probably don't. But Stony's kisses were firm without being hard—sweet and warm and wonderful. Stony's kisses were the kind I could definitely get used to!

As our lips parted, Stony looked up and pointed, not saying a word. I looked at the place where he was pointing, and there was the sun, a vivid orange ball, shyly peeking over the top of a distant mountain. The whole sky seemed to light up with orange and pink hues.

I found myself holding my breath, watching as the light slowly moved across the valley below, as if someone were pulling a dark blanket off a green carpet.

"Oh, Stony," I breathed reverently, deeply touched by the beauty of the scene unfolding before me. I was even more touched by the fact that he'd brought me up here to see this. He'd wanted to share this special place, this special sight, *with me!*

"I've been coming up here almost every summer morning for the past seven years," Stony said softly. "Before my dad died, he and I used to come here together, and we'd talk about someday owning that valley below, raising some horses." Stony smiled wistfully. "My dad was a dreamer, and I guess I'm a lot like him."

"There's nothing wrong with being a dreamer," I said, then touched his hand sympathetically. "How long ago did your dad die?"

"He died five years ago." His smile slowly faded and his expression turned reflective. "Dad was a great guy. He loved horses. He bought me my first pony when I was a year old." Stony turned his gaze back to the valley below. "Every year Dad, Mom, and I came here to Lake Vallecito for vacation, and Dad would talk a little more seriously about throwing in the towel in Durango and moving up here. But he died in a car accident before he got the chance. Mom hasn't been back to Hidden Ranch since Dad died. It's too painful for her to come here and face all the memories." Stony's eyes darkened. "I want to come back, though. This is where I spent the most time with my dad, and . . ." Suddenly he laughed self-consciously. "Sorry," he said, smiling apologetically. "I'm sure you don't want to hear about all this."

"But I do!" I protested, then I looked at him shyly. "I want to know everything there is to know about you."

He smiled at me gently, then reached out and traced a fingertip down my nose and across my mouth. "I feel the same way about you," he said.

"When did you start working here at Hidden Ranch?" I asked as his hand fell away from my face.

"The summer after my dad died. The Johnsons—they're the owners of the ranch and good friends of my parents—called my mom and suggested that maybe I'd like to come and work for them. I've been coming back here every summer since then."

"What exactly do you do at the ranch?" I

teased. "The only things I've seen you do is swim in the lake and cook hot dogs."

"Are you insinuating that I'm not a good worker?" Stony grinned at me.

"Not at all—you cooked those hot dogs to perfection!" I laughed.

"Well, I do have other duties. I'm in charge of the stables, and taking care of the horses. I lead all the organized trail rides. I do maintenance on the paddleboats and the fishing boats. I mend fences, pound nails, saw boards—whatever needs to be done, I do it." His expression brightened. "Oh, and the most important job I have here is public relations. I make sure all the girls are kept happy for the duration of their vacation."

Stony leaned forward and put his arms around me, his lips inches from mine. "That's the best part of my job," he murmured.

An unwanted thought of Julie pushed its way into my mind: Had she been "public relations" too?

I was determined to forget about Julie and enjoy this special moment with Stony. I leaned forward, enjoying the feel of his warm breath against my face. "And may I say, you do that part of your job very well," I managed to say before Stony's lips found mine.

"Someday I'm *going* to buy that valley down there and raise horses," Stony said after we'd kissed and were once again cuddled together, looking out at the scenery. "Just like my dad wanted."

I looked up at him, feeling my heart expand. "I think that's terrific," I said.

Stony looked down at me, giving me that crooked grin that made me feel so happy. "And I'm beginning to think you're pretty terrific!" he exclaimed. "Come on, let's take a ride. I've got a lot of things I want to show you!" He held out his hand to me, and with a happy laugh I let him pull me up.

If there was one complaint I had about the day, it was that it passed much too quickly. As the morning went by, I grew more and more comfortable on Sweetheart. The horse was gentle and rarely needed me to do anything with the reins.

At noon, we stopped by the edge of a small, swift-running stream where we could dangle our feet in the cool mountain water. Stony magically produced sandwiches and fruit from his saddlebag and we ate beneath a large pine tree, surrounded by chipmunks who all wanted to share our meal. After lunch, we lay on a grassy area next to the stream, talking as we basked in the warmth of the midday sun.

"Do you like to fish?" Stony asked, his eyes closed as he lay on his back next to me.

"Sure," I replied, hoping I didn't get struck by lightning as I told the little white lie. But I knew instinctively that Stony liked to fish, and I didn't want him to know I thought it was gross and boring.

"I'll have to take you fishing with me one day," Stony said.

"Okay," I responded, raising myself up on one elbow. I was glad his eyes were closed so that I could have a chance to just look at him. The sun was dancing in his light blond hair and his features were relaxed into a contented smile.

He's so good-looking, I thought, but my feelings for him were more than just physical attraction. He was so much fun, with his teasing, easy laughter. Also, I was impressed with his desire to carry out his father's dream.

I frowned as I suddenly thought about Julie again. I couldn't help but wonder what her relationship was with Stony, yet I didn't feel comfortable asking him about it. Whatever seemed to be bugging Julie about Stony seemed to be more than just plain old dislike.

Maybe I'm just imagining it, I thought to myself, laying back down and closing my eyes. *First Marcia told me I have a tendency to exaggerate things, then Jeff told me the same thing. Maybe that's what I'm doing now,* I thought, *exaggerating the fact that Julie doesn't like Stony and making it into something more than it really is.* I decided to dismiss the concern from my mind.

After all, whatever's going on between Julie and Stony doesn't have anything to do with me, I told myself.

"Are you sleeping?"

I opened my eyes to see Stony leaning on one elbow over me, smiling. "No," I answered. "Just thinking."

"What are you thinking about?" he asked.

"Oh, I don't know . . . I guess I was thinking it would be sort of nice if you lived in Denver," I answered, blushing slightly.

Stony's grin widened. "There's another one of those famous blushes."

I laughed and covered my cheeks with my hands. "I hate it when I blush!" I exclaimed.

Stony laughed. "I know what you mean. I have an eye that twitches horribly whenever I tell a lie."

"Really?" I sat up and looked at him seriously. "Which eye is it?" I asked, looking intently at both his blue eyes. Before he could answer, I nudged him in the ribs, realizing he was teasing me again. "You're so rotten," I laughed. "You really had me believing you!"

We got back on our horses, but I was disappointed when Stony suggested that we'd better call it a day. We walked our horses back to the stables, where we left them with a stable hand, then started walking to my cabin. Stony suddenly grew silent.

"Is something wrong?" I asked him.

"No, I was just thinking that I'm really going

to be sorry when your vacation ends and you have to go back to Denver," he said.

"Me, too," I agreed, not even wanting to think about it.

"Cat?" Stony stopped walking and turned to face me. "I know we haven't known each other very long, but . . . well, my mom goes to Denver all the time on buying trips. I've never gone with her, but now I'd like to, if I can see you there. Would it be all right if I got in touch with you?" he finished in a rush.

"*All right?*" I looked at him in amazement. "It would be more than all right," I replied. "Stony, I'd love for you to come and see me as often as you can!" I replied truthfully. *He likes me,* my heart sang. *He really likes me! This could be the beginning of a wonderful thing!*

"Great!" He smiled at me and took my hand as we began walking again. "Oh, there's one more thing," he said after a moment. "Would you call me Steve?"

I looked at him curiously. "Sure . . . but why? Don't you like your nickname?"

He grinned sheepishly. "Stony is what I'm called here at the ranch. It's sort of a nickname that I picked because it sounds macho, like a ranch worker's name. Stony is kind of an image I put on to please the guests." His brow wrinkled in frustration. "It's kind of hard to explain. All I can say is that I don't want you to be just another visitor who thinks of me as Stony. To you, I want to be Steve, like I am to all my friends back home."

"Okay, Steve," I said, happy that he wanted to tell me something like this about himself. Impulsively, I gave him a hug. "We'd better get back to the cabin, though—before Jeff decides to beat you up for keeping me out all day!"

"Come on." He grabbed my hand and tugged me along, pretending to be scared. "We'd better hurry!" Laughing, we both ran back to my cabin.

Chapter Eleven

I'm in love with Steve Mahoney.

These were the first words that came to mind the moment I woke up the next morning. I felt hot and cold, feverish and shivery, and I wanted to laugh and sing at the top of my lungs!

"Steve loves me," I whispered, hugging myself in delight. Sure, he hadn't exactly said those words. But he'd told me he wanted to spend every spare moment he had with me, and he'd told me that the first time he saw me he knew that I was going to be somebody special in his life. Surely that was as close to love as you could get!

I jumped up from my bed and headed for the shower stall. I knew Jeff was gone. When we'd gotten home last night, he and Stony had made plans to go fishing early this morning, so I had the cabin all to myself. I sang in the shower, filling the bathroom with the sounds of my happiness. When I was dressed, I went into the kitchen, realizing I was starving. I screamed in surprise as I saw Jeff sitting at the kitchen table.

"I thought you went fishing," I exclaimed.

"I did. I just got back a few minutes ago." Jeff grinned teasingly. "Just in time to hear your concerto in the shower. At first I thought it was a moose mating call."

"Cute, Jeff, real cute," I said dryly, reaching for the cinnamon rolls that were on the table. "So, did you catch any fish?" I asked, biting into one of the thickly iced rolls.

"A couple. Stony showed me how to bait the hook differently, and I think it made a big difference." Jeff gulped down some milk, then helped himself to another roll.

"Did he say anything about me?" I asked, licking my fingers and looking at him eagerly.

"Stony? Why would he want to talk about you?" Jeff asked, then snapped his fingers as if he'd suddenly remembered something. "He did say something about a big-mouth. I thought he was talking about a fish, but he could have been talking about you."

"What did you do, decide to become a stand-up comedian for the day?" I asked sarcastically.

"Actually, Stony did ask me a few questions about you," Jeff admitted, grabbing his third cinnamon roll.

"Like what?" I asked, sitting on the edge of the table.

Jeff took a bite and chewed exasperatingly slowly.

"Jeff!" I squealed impatiently, making him laugh loudly.

"Okay, okay! He just asked me if you had any boyfriends back home," Jeff answered.

"What did you tell him?" I asked.

"I told him that you'd never had a boyfriend in your life and he'd really be doing you a big favor if he'd be your boyfriend for just a little while."

I stared at Jeff in horror. "*You didn't,*" I gasped, immediately thinking of fifty ways I could kill my older brother.

"I didn't," Jeff admitted, and I breathed a sigh of relief. "Actually, I told him that you dated several guys but there was nobody really special."

I nodded thoughtfully. Jeff's second answer sounded a whole lot better than the first. "He also told me to tell you he should be around the paddleboats for a while this morning if you want to stop by there," Jeff added.

"Well, why didn't you say so sooner!" I said, jumping up so quickly that I knocked a chair to the floor. Jeff merely shook his head as I dashed out of the cabin.

There was a spring in my step as I ran toward the lake. Steve had asked Jeff about my boyfriends back home, another sure sign that he really cared about me!

When I reached the paddleboats, I was surprised to see a bunch of kids already on the dock.

"Kate!" Martha hurried over to me. "I was just going to come and get you!" She grinned. "A bunch of us are going paddleboating again today. Do you want to come with us?"

"Sure," I said, as I searched the shore for Stony—*Steve,* I corrected myself mentally. I looked beyond Martha and immediately spotted him talking to Julie, his blond hair gleaming in the sunlight. I got a funny feeling in my chest as I realized that they were arguing. Julie's face was red, and Steve's features were tense as they faced each other squarely. *What is going on with those two?* I wondered. Just then, Steve saw me and turned away from Julie. A smile lit up his face as he came toward me.

"Hi!" he said.

"Hi," I answered.

"Aren't you going paddleboating with the gang?" he asked.

"I think so. Actually, I didn't know they were going till I got here. I came down here to see you," I admitted. "Jeff told me you said you'd be down here for a while this morning."

"You almost missed me—I've got to get back to the stables for a trail ride." He smiled at me. "How about if we go fishing tonight after I get off work?"

I looked at him hesitantly. "Steve, you remember yesterday when I told you I liked to fish? Well, I lied," I confessed.

He grinned. "Have you ever actually caught a fish?" he asked.

"No," I admitted.

His grin widened. "That's why you hate fishing. Once you catch your first fish, you're hooked!" I giggled at his ridiculous pun.

I wanted to ask him about Julie, but just as the question formed on my lips, he looked at his watch and grimaced. "I've got to run," he said. "I'll come by your cabin later tonight and we'll fish," he added as he turned and ran toward the stables.

After he disappeared from sight, I turned back to the other kids. "Hey, that looks like fun!" I exclaimed as I stood on the dock watching as Sam and Johnny sat in one of the paddleboats, pedaling their feet furiously to move the boat away from the dock.

"Come on, Kate," Martha said excitedly. "We'll ride together!"

"I'll ride with Kate," Julie said suddenly, grabbing my arm and whisking me away from Martha. I don't know who was more surprised, Martha or me.

I glanced at her curiously as I sat down on the wide seat and put my feet on the pedals. She probably wanted to pump me for information about Jeff. But the image of Stony and Julie arguing just minutes before pushed its way into my mind and my stomach suddenly felt queasy.

Once Julie was settled down beside me, we began to pedal. "How do you turn these things?" I asked, trying to keep calm.

"If you want to go right, you pedal hard on the left side and don't pedal on the right side, and vice versa if you want to go left," Julie explained, laughing at my confused expression. "Don't worry about it; when it comes time for us to turn around, I'll show you what to do."

"Isn't this great?" Sam yelled from in front of us. He and Johnny were pedaling fast and furiously, moving quickly away from us.

"You think it's great now, but the way you guys are working your leg muscles, you won't be able to walk tomorrow," Julie said, laughing.

"What do you think we are, a couple of wimps?" Sam asked indignantly, pedaling even faster as he and Johnny sped away.

Julie and I laughed, keeping our own pedaling to an easy rhythm. "Are you enjoying your vacation?" Julie asked me.

"I'm having a fantastic time," I said happily.

"Actually, I wanted to ride with you because I wanted to talk to you," Julie said.

"About Jeff?" I asked.

"No . . . about Stony."

"What about Stony?" I could feel my heart

thudding in my chest. *Here it comes,* I thought. *Now I'll find out what's going on between the two of them. And it's probably something I'd have been better off not knowing.*

"I noticed the other night at the campfire that you two looked pretty cozy." Julie's eyes didn't quite meet mine.

"Is there some reason why I shouldn't be seeing Stony?" I asked her directly, unable to bear the suspense for one minute longer. *Oh, please don't tell me you and Stony are secretly engaged or something,* I prayed.

"The only reason you shouldn't get involved with Stony is because Stony is a creep!" Julie exclaimed. "Kate, Stony will break your heart if you don't watch out."

I laughed uneasily, wondering what on earth she was talking about. "I . . . I don't understand." I murmured, shaken by her harsh words. Julie looked at me intently. "Kate, Stony is an expert at making girls fall in love with him. He does it all summer long—it's just another part of his job!"

"You just don't like Stony," I answered indignantly. "It's been really obvious to me that you have some personal grudge against him!"

"I wouldn't like any guy who made it a practice of smooth-talking every girl who comes here during the summer," Julie exclaimed. "Stony is great at making a girl feel really special, but it doesn't mean anything—

it's all a big game to him! You've got to believe me."

I looked at her incredulously. I couldn't believe what she was saying. "Why are you telling me this?" I asked her.

"Because I like you and I like Jeff, and I don't want to see you get hurt by Stony," Julie answered without hesitation.

I laughed bitterly. "Julie, I don't know what you've got against Stony, but that's *your* problem," I said.

"It's your problem too!" Julie said, her face flushing. "He's doing the same thing to you that he's done to a dozen other girls! He'll make you fall in love with him, but when you leave here, he'll be sweet-talking the next new girl who arrives for a ten-day vacation!"

"I don't believe you!" I protested heatedly. *How dare she say these things about Stony,* I thought to myself. *How dare she tell me he doesn't care about me! I know he cares about me . . . I know he does!*

"Oh Kate, I know how terrific Stony appears to be, but it's all an act!"

"Then he deserves an Academy Award for the best acting in the world!" I said sarcastically. "Julie, I'm sorry that you don't like Stony, and I'm sorry that you don't think what he feels for me is real. But I know it's real! We spent the whole day together yesterday!"

"Let me guess—he took you to his secret

place and you watched a beautiful sunset together," Julie said. She stopped pedaling and gave me a knowing look.

I felt the blood drain from my face. "You don't know anything about the way Stony and I feel about each other," I whispered, but my mind was whirling. Apparently he'd taken Julie or somebody else up to his special place as well. "Believe me, I know all about Stony," Julie continued in a low voice, and when I looked at her, her eyes were filled with pain. "I know because last summer I was one of Stony's girls."

She grabbed my arm as I turned away from her and all the things she was saying—things I didn't want to hear. "Kate . . . I'm really sorry. I know this must hurt, but better that you get hurt sooner than later, when you care about Stony even more."

"I want to go back to the dock," I demanded.

She nodded, and we turned the paddleboat around. We didn't speak again as the boat moved swiftly through the water.

Stony took Julie up to his special place. He shared a sunset with her. Did he also tell her about his dad, and about his dreams of one day owning a piece of the valley? I wondered. *Did he tell her how much he missed his dad and how hard his dad's death had been on his mother?*

All the wonderful things he'd said to me couldn't be just words with no meaning be-

hind them! But what if he said those same things over and over again to dozens of girls all summer long?

No, it couldn't be true, I told myself. I couldn't believe that Stony didn't care about me. There had to be some explanation for the things Julie had told me. There had to be some kind of mistake.

When we reached the dock, I jumped out of the boat without saying another word to Julie. My heart told me that Stony really cared about me. But my head had a lot of questions that needed to be answered.

There is only one person who can answer my questions, I decided, *and that's Stony himself.*

Chapter Twelve

It was midafternoon when I finally decided to go search for Stony. I'd had a couple of hours to think about everything Julie had said, and I'd decided that I was doing the same thing Jeff and Marcia always told me I did—exaggerating the importance of things. Okay, so maybe Julie and Stony had seen each other last summer. That didn't mean that Stony was the total creep Julie had made him out to be. It sounded to me like she had a bad case of sour grapes.

I figured that what happened is that Stony and Julie dated, and Julie liked Stony, but Stony wasn't that crazy about Julie. *Now she's really jealous,* I told myself as I left our cabin and headed for the stables to find Stony. *She probably just made up a bunch of stuff about Stony and other girls because she didn't want to tell me that she still likes Stony and he doesn't like her.*

The first place I looked for him was in the stables, but he wasn't there. Manny, his big black horse, was in his stall, so I knew Stony had returned from the trail ride. The next place I looked was the shed where the boats were stored. The small shed by the dock was empty, however, and Stony was nowhere to be found.

I started back to our cabin, thinking that I'd be seeing him this evening anyway, because he was taking me fishing. The more I thought about everything, the better I was feeling. "Stony cares about me and nothing anyone can say will make me feel any different!" I muttered as I cut through the woods near the main office building. I was walking around the main office when I caught a glimpse of white-blond hair just outside the office door. Knowing in my heart that Julie was all wrong about Stony, I sneaked around the side of the building, intent on surprising him. I moved around the building and peeked around the corner, pausing as I realized he was talking to somebody. *I'll wait until he's finished with his conversation,* I thought.

"So, where are you from?" I could hear Stony's voice perfectly from the corner of the building. *He's talking to a new guest,* I thought.

"We're from St. Louis, Missouri," a female voice answered.

I peeked out from behind the wall to get a

good look at the girl Stony was talking to. She sounded pretty young from her voice. My eyes widened when I saw the blond, shapely girl Stony was talking to. Nothing could have prepared me for the jealousy I felt. She was dressed in tight cropped jeans and a lacy pink sleeveless top, and she was looking up at Stony as if he were the greatest thing since sliced bread.

"Missouri, huh? I'll have to visit there soon if they grow all the girls as pretty as you," Stony said. As I watched, he gave the blond girl a slow, lazy smile—the very same smile that always made my knees feel like Jell-O.

I leaned back against the building and clapped my hands over my ears, not wanting to hear one more lying word from his lips. *He said exactly the same words to me when we first met,* I told myself angrily. *He doesn't care for me at all! I'm just another one of his summer diversions, another female guest to keep happy!* The pain that ripped through my insides at this thought left me breathless. I bit my bottom lip so hard I actually tasted blood.

"So, do you work here?" asked the blond girl, for whom I'd developed an instant hatred.

"Yeah, it's sort of my job to keep all the blond, blue-eyed girls happy while they're here," Stony said.

"And I'll bet you're very good at it!" the blond girl replied, and I could tell by her voice that she was blatantly flirting with him.

I'm not even gone yet, and already he has a replacement all picked out. "Julie's right," I whispered painfully, squeezing my eyelids tightly closed and biting down on my bottom lip. *Oh Stony,* my heart cried, *how could you?*

I turned and ran blindly into the woods, tears burning at my eyes as I choked back sob after sob.

I was grateful that Jeff was gone when I got back to the cabin. I wanted to be alone in my miserable state.

There is medicine for headaches and stomachaches, so you'd think some scientist would have been able to come up with a cure for heartache by now, I thought bitterly as I wandered around the empty cabin.

How am I going to get through the next four days without falling apart every time I see him? I asked myself. "I just won't see him," I said aloud defiantly, thinking of the days ahead of me before we'd leave for Denver. "I'll just stay right here in this cabin for the next four days," I told myself firmly. But the cabin had no television, no radio, nothing to help me pass the time while I hid out from Stony. I could hide somewhere in the woods and read. I couldn't stand it if I had to see Stony again and look into his mesmerizing blue eyes.

I jumped as somebody knocked on the cabin

door. I stood still, grateful that I was in a part of my bedroom where nobody could see me. I didn't feel like seeing or talking to anyone right now.

"Kate? Jeff? Anyone in there?"

My heart skipped a few beats at the sound of Stony's voice. A few seconds later I heard his receding footsteps and I breathed a sigh of relief. I leaned weakly against the bedroom wall, fighting the impulse to cry once again. I stiffened suddenly as I heard the door to our cabin open. Had he come back? I peeked into the kitchen and sighed when I saw that it was only Jeff.

"Hey, what are you doing here?" Jeff asked in surprise as I came into the kitchen.

"I live here," I answered glumly. "At least until this horrible vacation is over."

Jeff just looked at me. "I just saw Stony and he asked me where you were. He said he'd just been here and the cabin was empty."

"I didn't want to see him. In fact, I don't ever want to see him again," I said passionately.

"Uh oh, sounds like a lovers' quarrel to me," Jeff said with a small smile. "Take it from an experienced guy—it's always better to talk out a problem instead of ignoring it." He opened up the refrigerator and grabbed a can of soda.

"Stony and I have nothing to talk about. We don't have any problems and we didn't have a fight. I just never want to see or talk to him again!" I exclaimed, unable to keep the hurt and anger out of my voice.

"Whew," Jeff whistled as he sat down at the kitchen table and looked at me curiously. "Do you want to talk about it?"

I shook my head, my chin quivering. No amount of talk was going to change the fact that Stony had lied to me. He was nothing but a smooth-talking creep! "No, just do me a favor. If Stony comes around here looking for me, tell him I'm not here—or tell him I got married!" I said, fighting back the sting of unshed tears burning in my eyes.

"Are you sure, Kate?" Jeff looked at me seriously, his brown eyes filled with sympathy.

I nodded. "I'm perfectly sure."

"Okay, if that's the way you want it," he agreed softly.

No, I felt like screaming, *that's not the way I want it!* Instead, I nodded and went into my bedroom, where I could allow my unshed tears to fall freely.

"I'm sorry, she doesn't want to talk to you," Jeff told Stony when he came by the cabin later that evening. My bedroom door was open a crack and my ear was pressed up against it as I listened to their conversation.

"What do you mean? We have a fishing date." I heard Stony laugh. "Come on, Jeff, would you tell Kate I'm here?"

"Stony, I'm not joking. Kate really doesn't

want to talk to you," Jeff replied, joining Stony out on the sun deck and closing the cabin door behind him.

Drat! Now I couldn't hear them! I opened my bedroom door and crawled on my hands and knees across the kitchen floor, stopping beneath the window that faced the sun deck. The window was open and I could hear their conversation perfectly, although my left foot was already growing numb from lack of circulation as I crouched awkwardly beneath the window.

"I don't know what happened between you two, but she says she never wants to see you or talk to you again," I heard Jeff explaining.

"This is crazy! Nothing happened between us!" I almost laughed out loud at Stony's incredulous disbelief. *Oh right, he hasn't done anything*, I said to myself. *He's just played me for a complete fool!*

"Come on, Jeff, just let me come in and talk to her so I can find out what's going on," Stony persisted.

Jeff hesitated, and my heart stood still. Surely he wasn't thinking of giving in to him? I shifted positions, getting ready to run into the bedroom if Jeff decided to let him in.

"Stony, I really like you, and if this thing with Kate is some sort of mistake I'm really sorry and I hope you find a way to resolve it, but I can't let you come in. I promised Kate that I wouldn't," he said.

There was a moment of silence and I grabbed my left foot, rubbing it roughly to get rid of the pins-and-needles sensation. I stopped rubbing as Stony spoke again.

"I just can't figure this out. She didn't tell you anything about why she's mad at me?" Jeff must have shook his head, because Stony continued. "I just saw her this morning, and everything was fine."

"Look Stony, I'll try to get Kate to talk to you, but I can't make any promises. Kate can be pretty stubborn," Jeff said sympathetically.

What a creep! I thought, pinching my foot angrily. I could tell by Jeff's voice that he was sorry for Stony and thought I was being silly. Did guys always stick together no matter who was right or who was wrong?

"Okay, thanks, Jeff," Stony answered. I heard him leave, and Jeff came back inside. He jumped back, startled, when he saw me crouched beneath the window.

"You heard the whole thing?" he asked.

I nodded.

"Kate, don't you think you owe it to the guy to at least tell him what he's done wrong?" Jeff asked, glancing at me impatiently. "He looked pretty miserable when he left just now."

"He probably practiced his look of misery a dozen times in front of his mirror to make sure he had it right," I retorted angrily. "Steve Mahoney is nothing but a fake!"

Chapter Thirteen

"We're all going to the Double O Saloon tonight for dinner and some dancing. That means you, too, Kate." Mom looked at me sternly. "You've been moping around here ever since your father and I got back from Durango two days ago."

I flushed, but said nothing. Mom and Dad thought I was still pouting because we'd spent our vacation here instead of in California. It was easier for me to let them think that than to explain what was really wrong with me. I didn't want my folks to know I was stupid enough to have my heart broken by a vacation romance.

"We'll be leaving here early in the morning to go back home, so tonight is the last night of our vacation and I want us all to have a good time," Mom continued, looking at me pointedly.

I nodded. I'd been successful in dodging

Stony for the past three days. Even if he did show up at the Double O Saloon, we'd be surrounded by people and it would be impossible for us to talk privately.

I picked at the fried fish on my plate, absently listening as Mom and Dad told Jeff about the train ride they'd taken in Durango. It really hadn't been too difficult for me to avoid Stony. Of course, I hadn't left the cabin much in the past three days. Martha had come over several times, so she knew the whole story.

"Don't you think so, Kate?" Mom looked at me expectantly and I blushed, realizing I hadn't heard a word of the conversation going on around me.

"I'm sorry, I wasn't paying attention," I answered.

"Honestly, Kate, you have been a total space cadet since we got back from Durango." Mom sighed impatiently. "If I didn't know better, I'd swear you were in love. But people in love usually have a smile on their faces, and you look like I don't know what!"

A sob suddenly escaped from my throat at my mom's words. I jumped up from the table and ran to my room.

"What did I say?" I heard Mom ask Jeff and Dad as I slammed my bedroom door and threw myself down on the bed.

A few minutes later, Mom knocked softly on my door. "Kate, honey, can I come in?"

"Okay," I sighed resignedly, knowing Mom would probably want an explanation, and I couldn't blame it on the fact that we hadn't gone to California on vacation. That just wasn't fair to my parents.

Mom sat down on the edge of my bed and looked at me, gently pushing a strand of hair off my forehead. "Jeff explained to us that you and Stony were sort of seeing each other, then something happened between you and you've been real upset. Honey, why didn't you tell me?"

"There's nothing to tell," I said bitterly. "I was stupid and I fell for a smooth line and a handsome face—but that's all Stony is."

"It's funny, I didn't get that sort of impression when I talked to Stony. He seemed to be a bright, sincere young man," Mom said.

"You see, he fooled you, too!" I sat up and looked at Mom in frustration. "Mom, Stony made me feel different than any guy ever made me feel," I continued. "He made me feel like I was the most important girl in the world to him."

"That's a nice quality for a boy to have," Mom commented.

"Even if he acts that way to every other girl he meets?" I asked her incredulously.

"Oh," Mom said, finally seeming to understand. She was silent for a moment, then she looked at me with a small smile. "Kate, there are a lot of different kinds of men in the world. Some are shy; some are boisterous; and then there are some who seem to enjoy wooing a girl and making her fall in love with him. Everyone has a guy like that in her life at one time or another, a guy who makes you feel like you're the most beautiful woman in the world."

"Did you?" I asked, sitting up and looking at her expectantly.

"Yes, I did." Mom smiled softly, her eyes hazy with memories. "He was so handsome, and he'd send me flowers and write me love poems that didn't rhyme and were kind of corny, but at the time I thought they were the most romantic things I'd ever read."

"What happened to him?" I asked.

Mom smiled, her eyes shining brightly. "I got lucky. I married him."

"Dad?" I asked in amazement, finding it hard to believe my father had ever written a poem, let alone a love poem.

Mom nodded and laughed out loud. "Your father was quite a smooth one in his day." She leaned over and kissed me on the forehead. "Now why don't you get up and get dressed real pretty and we'll all go to the Double O and have a good time." She stood up and walked over to the bedroom door, then turned back and looked at me. "Kate, some day you'll find a guy who makes you feel like you're the most special girl in his life, and it'll last a lifetime. Someday you'll find the guy who's just right for you." With this, she turned and closed my door, leaving me alone.

I sat for a moment, thinking about what Mom had said. Somehow her words didn't make me feel any better. I'd already found the guy who was just right for me—the problem was I wasn't right for him. With a deep sigh, I got up and got dressed for the last night of our vacation.

The Double O was packed when we walked in. As we sat down in a booth, I looked over to the dance floor. Had it only been four nights ago that Stony held me in his arms and taught me how to do the two-step? Had it only been four nights ago that I thought I'd found the boy of my dreams, a fantasy come to life?

I was grateful to see as I looked around the room that there was no blond-haired, blue-eyed guy here. *Maybe he's taken that new girl up to his special place to see the sunset,* I thought bitterly.

"Let's dance," Dad said to Mom, and they got up and went out onto the dance floor.

"Are you okay?" Jeff asked me, and I smiled at him. I'd been pretty hateful to him the past couple of days, and I figured it was time to start acting like a human being again.

"Yeah, I'm okay," I lied.

"You wanna dance?" he asked, looking relieved when I shook my head. Jeff was great on the football field, but he was a total klutz on the dance floor, so he rarely, if ever, danced.

"Kate! Hey, Kate!" came Martha's voice.

I looked around the crowd, trying to find Martha in the sea of people. I finally spotted her across the room, waving to me frantically. "When Mom and Dad get back to the table, tell them I went to sit with Martha," I said to Jeff. Then I got up and made my way to where Martha was sitting with her family.

When I reached their table, Martha immediately jumped up and grabbed my arm, steering me to a small empty table at the back of the bar.

"So, you finally decided to end your hibernation," she exclaimed, giving my arm a friendly squeeze.

Martha had come by the cabin two days ago and I'd told her everything. "Mom and Dad forced me out because it's our last night here."

"Your last night!" Martha wailed. "Jeez, it seems like you just got here!"

I didn't answer that. To me, it seemed like I'd been here forever, especially after the past four days.

"You'll come back next year, won't you?" Martha urged.

"Oh, I don't think so," I said. *If Mom and Dad insist we come back here next year, I'm hopping a freighter to Alaska!* I thought.

"You've got to come back—you're one of us now, the KFFers."

"I don't know; we'll just have to wait and see," I answered noncommittally. "Though I really will miss you, Martha. You've been a great friend these past few days."

"Well, maybe we can write—"

"Kate."

I looked up, my breath catching in my throat as I saw Stony standing at our table. Darn, darn, *darn!* This wasn't supposed to happen!

'Kate, would you dance with me?" Stony asked.

I looked at him coolly, trying not to notice how handsome he looked in a denim-blue, Western-cut shirt and a pair of faded jeans and boots. "I really don't feel like dancing," I said, forcing my gaze toward Martha.

"Kate . . . please." Stony laid his hand on my shoulder.

"I said I don't want to dance!" I snapped. I blushed when I realized that my raised voice had drawn the attention of people at the surrounding tables.

"I'm not going to leave here until you dance with me," Stony said, a stubborn look on his handsome face.

"Go on, Kate, dance with him before you make a scene," Martha said.

I nodded and stood up. *I'll dance with you, but I won't talk to you,* I vowed as he took my hand and led me out to the dance floor. I stiffened woodenly as his arms went around me and he began to move to the sounds of the mellow country song.

I tried to ignore the way my heart beat rapidly at the sensation of his arms around me. I tried to divert my attention from the smell of his cologne, and from the way the overhead lights made his blond hair glitter.

"Kate, what's been going on?" His breath was warm in my ear. As he looked down into my eyes, I looked away, refusing to meet his gaze. "Tell me!" he demanded. "I thought we had something special between us. Why are you doing this to me?"

"Why am *I* doing this to *you*?" I jerked out of his arms and looked at him incredulously. "That's great, that's just great! You play all kinds of games with my emotions. You make me think you really care about me! You make me think we have a chance at some kind of a real relationship, but it's all lies, all stupid lies! You're a fake, Stony. A big fake!"

I turned away from him and ran for the nearest exit. I was losing all the self-control I'd worked at for the past four days, and I was soon sobbing frantically. I ran out of the Double O, but didn't stop there. I ran through the woods, wanting to put as much distance between me and Stony as possible. I didn't want him to see how badly he'd hurt me. He was such a creep—it would probably only feed his ego.

I came to a stop when I reached the edge of the lake. I found a flat rock and sat down, letting my tears flow freely down my cheeks. I was exhausted. For four days I'd been trying to control my worry about seeing Stony, and now all I felt was exhaustion.

It was a beautiful summer night, warm with a comfortable breeze. The moon was full, shining brilliantly on the water. Summer nights . . . summer love . . . How had a simple fishing vacation ended with me sitting by the edge of a lake crying for a guy who was a heartless jerk?

"Kate?"

I closed my eyes and breathed a deep sigh. "Go away, Stony. Please just go away."

"I can't." My eyes were still closed, but I felt his presence as he sat down next to me on the rock. "I can't just go away. All the things you said back there, about me being a liar and all. I don't understand, Kate."

I opened my eyes and looked at him, my heart aching. He was so handsome . . . but it was only skin-deep, I reminded myself. "Stony, what do you want from me?" I asked. "Do you want to make sure that you broke my heart?" I sighed miserably, wiping at my tears. "Okay, you broke my heart. There, now you can move on to the next pretty visitor to Lake Vallecito."

"What are you talking about?" Stony asked impatiently, grabbing hold of my shoulders.

For a moment I thought he was going to shake me. "I feel like you're talking in riddles. When have I lied to you? I don't get it. How have I broken your heart?"

"You took me up to your secret place, and you made me believe that I was the only girl you'd ever had up there. Then I found out that last summer you took Julie up there!" I blurted out angrily, shaking his hands off my shoulders. "How many other girls have you taken up there, Stony?"

Stony sighed and ran a hand through his hair in frustration. "I knew I should have straightened out this thing with Julie," he said, more to himself than to me. "There has been nobody else up on that bluff, nobody but you and Julie."

I looked at him dubiously, but kept my mouth shut and allowed him to continue. "Kate, last summer Julie was the last of the kids to go home. We spent a lot of time together and I guess Julie got the wrong idea. I mean, I liked her as a friend, but I guess she thought. . . . Sure, I took her up there to the bluff one evening. But I didn't kiss her, and I didn't tell her the things I told you. I shared my special place with Julie because she was a friend. I shared it with you for a different reason."

I looked away from him, focusing on the reflection of the full moon on the water. "You know what I think? I think you have such a smooth line, you don't know when you're lying and when you're not."

"That's not true," Stony protested, sounding wounded.

"You're from Denver?" I mimicked. "I'll have to visit there some time if they grow all the girls as pretty as you," I finished sarcastically. "You said that to me when we first met, and I thought you really meant it. Then the other morning, I heard you saying it to another girl, and that's when I realized you're nothing but a smooth line and a bunch of lies."

In the brilliance of the moonlight I saw him blush. "You're right," he said, his shoulders slumping. His words should have made me feel triumphant, but instead they only caused another stab of pain to shoot through me. "Kate," he said, taking my hand in his. When I tried to pull it away, he held on even more tightly. "You're absolutely right: I've developed a smooth line of talk just for the girls who come to this resort. But Kate, that isn't me, that's Stony! I'm Steve, and I tried to tell you that the night we walked home from the Double O. Stony has a smooth line—it's part of his job to be real friendly to the girls who come here." He sighed, pressing his fingers against his temples. "When I first met you, I met you as Stony, and I used all of Stony's lines, but that morning when we shared the sunrise, I wanted you to see me as Steve. I told you things Stony had never told anyone. As I got to know you that day, I realized I was really growing to care about you, more than I'd ever cared for a girl before in my life. I may have met you as Stony, but I fell in love with you as Steve!"

My heart leapt in my chest, suddenly alive and kicking once again. Still, I was hesitant. "You can't be two people at the same time. I can't hate Stony and love Steve. They're both a part of you," I explained.

"Not anymore," Stony said, his eyes glistening in the moonlight. "I'm retiring Stony as of right now. I don't want to be Stony; I want to be Steve. The guy who you grew to like." Steve raised my hand and held it to his lips. "Kate, I've been working up here for several summers, and I've never met a girl who made me want to forget everything else—except you."

I was trembling, and I realized that I believed him. Nobody, not even the greatest actor in the world, could look at me the way he was looking at me and not care about me. The truth was there in his eyes, and my heart made a sudden, miraculous recovery.

"Oh, Steve," I murmured softly, leaning toward him, wanting to feel his arms around me.

I snuggled against him as he put his arms around me. "You know, I have a feeling my mom is going to be making a lot of trips to

Denver over the next year. And I suddenly have a strong desire to see the sights there," he said with the little crooked smile that made my heart dance.

"I can recommend a very good guide," I said, smiling up at him.

"In fact, I have a feeling it's going to take me every weekend for the next ten years to see everything Denver has to offer."

"Every weekend?" I asked hopefully.

"You bet. Especially if they grow all the girls as pretty as you." He leaned down, and his lips found mine. All around us the summer night was alive with sounds, and the breeze caressed us as we clung together.

I kissed him back fervently, thinking how happy I was that I had followed my heart.

Sweet
Dreams

First Kiss

SWEET VALLEY HIGH

Super Star

A sensational new spin-off series of titles, each highlighting one specific character from Jessica and Elizabeth's friends at Sweet Valley High!

1. LILA'S STORY SBN 0 553 401297
2. BRUCE'S STORY SBN 0 553 401300